I0684395

# Burning Wild
## Sexy
## Stories
## Collection

## VOLUME 2

### 10 EROTIC SHORT STORIES

## CANDRA AUBREY

Burning Wild/ Candra Aubrey -- 1st ed.
Xplicit Press, an imprint of TLM Media LLC

ISBN-13: 978-1-62327-525-9
ISBN-10: 1-62327-525-3
eISBN: 978-1-62327-583-9

Printed in the United States of America

# CONTENTS

# 1 BURNING UP

Desiree Nyman liked virgins. They tasted the best, their energy pure and untainted by the flavoring that came with sex. They were the scent of the air after a warm summer rain. The one currently writhing on the bed beneath her was no different. Fisher Whyte was a nineteen year-old engineering major with dark blond hair, warm brown eyes and cute, wire-rimmed glasses. He enjoyed science fiction, running, and had a nice singing voice. Unlike others of her kind, Desiree liked to get to know her meal. Not well enough for a relationship, mind you, but enough that she felt more human than succubus.

"Please, please," Fisher begged, hands fisting in his sheets, eyes darkened to almost black with lust and need.

Desiree placed her hand in the center of his chest, reveling in his pounding heart. Energy pulsed through her, every cell humming and crackling as the powerful muscles in her legs moved her. Her auburn hair was damp with sweat, her fair skin flushed and glistening. She'd been feeding her own life force into him for the past ten minutes, lengthening what could've been a brief encounter, but she was ready now.

She dropped down onto him, internal muscles squeezing as he cried out and emptied himself into her. As his seed flowed into her, with it came the energy she needed to survive. It washed over her, triggering her own climax. Her nails scraped against his chest and her head fell back. She closed her eyes, knowing her normally smoky blue irises would be glowing like sapphires as her body absorbed the sexual energy Fisher had released. Desiree let herself fall forward, resting her cheek against Fisher's chest. Her full breasts pressed against his flat stomach and she felt him shrinking inside her.

"Thank you," Fisher's voice was still breathless. One hand tentatively brushed back some of Desiree's hair.

"My pleasure," she replied, rolling off of him. She bent over him, pressing her lips against his in a surprisingly chaste kiss. "And I mean that literally." She chuckled, her voice low and husky. "I've got to run." She climbed out of bed, reaching for her clothes.

"Will I see you around campus?" Fisher rolled onto his side, eyes bright.

Desiree gave him a soft smile. That was the only problem with virgins: sometimes they got attached. "No, I'm leaving in the morning." She ran her fingers through Fisher's hair, refraining from licking her lips at the delightful charge running up her arm. A light push of power and Fisher's eyes began to close. "Sleep, darling boy. You've earned it." His breathing had been already heavy and deep by the time Desiree brushed her lips across his forehead.

It was still dark when Desiree slipped out of the dorm room, but she could smell the sun creeping towards the horizon. Her body sang with magic, and it was all she could do to keep from skipping. Fisher had been a true treat. Rarely was one of this century so sweet and uncorrupted.

Desiree stopped at the edge of the woods to slip off her shoes. Heels were great for seduction, not so much for traipsing through a forest in the wee hours of the morning. The ground was cool beneath her feet and she could feel the coming cold. It would snow in

Michigan before week's end. She shivered. Succubae were creatures of heat and desire. The only time she liked snow was when she had warm bodies around her. But, she had one more thing to do in the chilly northeast before heading for warmer parts.

A foot into the trees and Desiree side-stepped into Central Park. She wrinkled her nose against the stench of steel and exhaust and the sheer volume of humanity. Like most of her kind, she wasn't overly fond of technology, but she understood it better than others and had built up a tolerance so that even a few hours didn't bother her. As long as she left before noon, she would be fine. Based on the amount of magic she'd be using in the next couple hours, she would need to refuel again, too, or she'd end up drained by the time she reached her next destination. Fortunately, her task would allow her to kill two birds with one stone, so to speak.

She started out on foot, wanting to enjoy her delightful little snack a while longer before she burned it away. She'd known hunger for far too long to not relish the delightful sensation of being full with something so... yummy. When she'd first been created – a human turned by a fey into something not quite of faerie but no longer of man – the world had frowned on anyone expressing a desire for sex, much less a woman. She'd fought her true nature for centuries, depriving herself of what she needed until, driven by a hunger that nearly drove her mad, she would drain strangers dry, leaving a dry husk blown to dust in the wind. As time passed, she gained control so that she no longer killed her food, but she still starved herself to avoid the stigma associated with a woman with 'loose morals.' She shied away from others of her kind, seeing them as the monsters she imagined herself to be. If she'd known how, she would have ended her life.

Everything had changed when she'd met Dean, an incubus who had been one of the original of their kind. The first fey had changed him in a time when the skins between the worlds had been thinner. He was as beautiful when Desiree had met him as he had been on the day he'd transitioned from man to incubus, and, she supposed, he looked the same now and would still in another thousand years. Dean had been the first of her kind to show her that feeding didn't have to be rough and dirty, something to be ashamed of. He taught her that it wasn't wrong to bring pleasure to the ones she fed from, that it wasn't wrong to gain pleasure from the power. They had stayed together for two centuries before going their own ways and Desiree had seen the world with new eyes since.

As the twentieth century passed its midway point, she left Europe for America, embracing the newly found freedom of its people. She still traveled back to the land of her birth and visited the places she'd come to love over the thousands of years she'd been alive, but, for the past fifty years, the United States had been her home. Walking through Central Park, she felt a deep love for her adopted country swell inside and smiled.

She chose a nice hotel, charming the check-in clerk into giving her a room free of charge. After all, she only intended to use it for a few hours. She took some time to enjoy the spacious shower and ended up on the king-sized bed, fluffy white robe tied around her waist as the sun finally peeked over the horizon.

"Now, let's get started," Desiree closed her eyes, reaching out with her magic. She held the images in her mind, faces she'd only seen when she connected with Fisher. Ilias Mann and Boone Cooper were both a year ahead of Fisher in high school and both had made his life miserable. They'd come to New York after graduation; Boone to pursue a career in theater, Ilias to play in an indoor soccer league. They'd fallen out of touch, but Desiree intended to rectify that. Both men were still asleep when she located them, their minds open and vulnerable to her Puck-like intentions. After implanting memories of a wild night of debauchery, she wrapped her metaphysical hands around each of them and yanked them through the folds of space. In an instant, she had two very handsome, very naked, young men next to her, one on either side.

Ilias was tall and lean, yards of toned muscles. He had a strong face under short red curls. His skin was fair and freckled, and Desiree knew that when he opened his eyes, they'd be an arrogant hazel. Boone was shorter, just under six feet with a similar build, though he was softer than Ilias. His hair was dark brown, his eyes light green and his face almost too pretty for a boy.

"Time to rise and shine." Desiree ran a finger down Ilias's cheek first, then Boone, slowing drawing them from dreams she'd placed in their minds. Bare limbs entwined. Lips and teeth and tongue. The taste of salt and sweat. The smell of sex and candy. Desiree had a sudden craving for chocolate.

Ilias woke first and he smiled lazily up at her. She heard Boone stirring on her other side and grinned in anticipation. It was Ilias's stretch that made both men realize that she wasn't the only one in the bed. She chuckled at their startled yelps and watched both scramble out of bed. She loosened the tie on her robe, thoroughly uninterested in the sounds of protests they both were making. She parted the robe, exposing her body to the cool air.

"Excuse me," she purred, her voice rippling with power. "Last night you boys promised me a second round." Two astonished faces turned her way. "Or aren't you up for that?"

Ilias acted first, as she'd known he would. He sauntered towards the bed, gaze devouring her naked body. She knew how she looked and ran a finger over her full lips. Her appearance hadn't changed since she'd transitioned, still curvy with heavy breasts and the perfect swell of hips. The hair between her legs was sparse and red.

"I'm up for anything." His voice dripped with ego.

Desiree's smile widened. "I'm so glad." She kept her voice sugary sweet. "You guys fell asleep before we could get to the real fun."

Ilias and Boone exchanged glances before looking back at Desiree. They knelt on the bed near her feet, careful to keep each other at arm's length. Desiree slid her finger into her mouth, hollowing her cheeks as she sucked on it. Blood rushed downwards and two cocks sprang to attention. Ilias was long and thin, rising straight up from reddish-brown curls. Boone was about one inch shorter but wider, his dick curving slightly at the end.

"Do I still get to be in charge?" Desiree ran her finger down the valley between her breasts, watching the men's eyes following it.

Two heads bobbed without hesitation and Desiree breathed, "Excellent."

A succubae's magic was elemental, drawing from innate desire, whether acknowledged or not. She couldn't force someone to behave in a way that truly went against what they wanted but, if they gave her control, she could use her power to eliminate doubts and erase inhibitions. These two were prime examples.

"Kiss for me." Desiree's voice was soft, but both men jumped as if she'd shouted. She feigned confusion. "You did it last night."

Boone's face drained of color even as Ilias's flooded red.

"Don't you remember?" Desiree parted her legs and dipped her finger between her folds. "I sure do. Watching the two of you got me so wet. And then, when you went down on each other," she moaned, pumping her finger slowly in and out, "I came so hard."

Ilias swallowed hard, throat convulsing, and stole a glance at his old friend. Boone's hand had dropped to his erection, fingers barely touching himself.

Desiree gave a fake pout. "Come on. You promised I could be in charge and you said I could have anything I wanted." She pushed power at the men and waited.

Boone moved first this time. He caught Ilias by the back of the neck and yanked the younger man towards him.

Desiree whimpered as the surge of repressed longing washed over her. These two may have claimed one hundred percent heterosexuality, but they'd been lusting after each other for years and the flavor of them proved it. If Fisher had been the light summer rain, these two were spicy sandalwood and shadows. And with the strength of energy pouring off of them from just one kiss, Desire knew after this encounter, she would be sated for a month. And what a kiss! Neither had any prior experience kissing men, that much was obvious. Teeth crashed against teeth and both fought for dominance.

Desiree sighed. She hated to rush things, but she was all too aware of the sun creeping higher and higher in the sky. As she used her magic, she could feel the steel and metal closing around her. Time to move things along.

She considered both men for a moment, debating which one she wanted inside her. One of Fisher's memories floated forward and she made her decision. After all, there was more than one way for a succubus to feed. She wanted neither one coming away from the encounter justifying it by saying at least they'd been in a woman.

"I know what I want now." She put power behind her words, knowing her eyes had started to glow. The men turned towards her, expressions slightly dazed. They didn't even seem aware that they were still touching each other. She crooked a finger at Ilias and spread her legs wider. "Let's put that tongue to good use."

Ilias grinned and scrambled up between Desiree's legs. She put a hand on his shoulder before he could lower himself. She wanted to see the expression on his face when she said the next part. Plus, the contact would help her remove any of his lingering reservations. "While Ilias is eating me out, I want Boone to fuck his ass."

She wished she could have taken a

picture of both men at that moment and sent it to Fisher. His former tormenters had myriad emotions flash across their faces. Disbelief. Denial. And, finally, desire. Not just desire for her, but for each other, for the culmination of years of harboring wants. She couldn't resist the temptation. "And I want to hear Ilias ask for it."

Male pride warred with the need for release, but as Ilias's swollen member hadn't flagged at the thought of Boone fucking him, Desiree knew she'd win. She wasn't disappointed.

"Please, Boone," Ilias dropped his eyes to Desiree's cunt. He bent at the waist, lowering his head to just the right height while keeping his ass up in the air. "I want you to fuck me."

Boone made a low noise in the back of his throat, whether from the words or from the sight of his friend's firm buttocks, legs partially spread in invitation, Desiree wasn't sure. It didn't matter though because, at that moment, Ilias pressed his mouth against her, tongue delving between her folds, lapping up the moisture that had gathered there. He sucked her clit into his mouth, teasing it with the tip of his tongue. Suddenly, he jumped, every muscle in his body tightening.

Desiree took her eyes from the redhead between her legs and looked behind him.

She grinned as she saw just the top of Boone's dark head. His face was buried between Ilias's cheeks and, based on the renewed thrusting of Ilias's tongue into her pussy, she could guess what Boone was doing. She let the sensation of Ilias's ministrations flood her, but kept her gaze fixed on Boone. After a few minutes, he straightened, eyes still focused on Ilias's asshole. His hand moved and Ilias made a noise that Desiree's cunt muffled. When Boone's hand began to move, she knew that he had a finger inside his friend. A drawn out groan soon indicated that a second had been added.

Desiree flicked a finger towards Boone and he looked down to see a bottle of lube. He didn't need any further prompting to withdraw his fingers and liberally coat his aching cock. Desiree felt her cells starting to hum and she opened her mind to the two men with her, letting their thoughts and emotions wash over and around her. She could taste herself on Ilias's tongue, feel the texture of her silken walls against his taste buds. She felt the pain of initial penetration as Boone started to ease his way inside his friend, felt the tight heat of Ilias's ass around Boone's cock, and felt Boone struggle not to force himself deeper. She placed a hand on Ilias's hair, lightly scratching at his scalp, using her magic to relax his muscles enough to let Boone push forward until his balls rested against Ilias.

"Now," she practically growled, tearing down the barriers that separated the men.

Boone pulled back and Ilias whimpered at the pleasurable burn. When his hips snapped forward, the whimper turned into a keen that sent an orgasm racing through Desiree's entire body. The sound triggered something in Boone and he began to pound into Ilias, driving the younger man's face against Desiree's cunt with such force that Ilias could do little more than keep his tongue out and let it dip just inside her core with each thrust. Desiree could feel a second climax coming and knew that she needed them to cum with her. The sun was growing too close to its zenith and she needed the men's energy soon.

She closed her eyes and arched her back, shifting her hips enough that Ilias's questing tongue jabbed against her clit at the exact moment she released the part of her that made her a succubus. Boone came with a grunt, pumping his seed into Ilias's ass.

"Fuck," Ilias cried out as his cum splattered across the bedspread.

Desiree's mouth opened in a silent scream as wave after wave of energy roiled over her. It was almost too much, too soon, after Fisher and she dug her nails into Ilias's shoulder, drawing more and more power from the men until the room shone with the glow of her skin. Fortunately, Ilias and Boone had collapsed on the bed, eyes closed, and didn't see the glimpse of what Desiree truly was. She shuddered as her body absorbed everything, her breathing calming and her heart returning to its normal rate. Even after her glow had faded, it took her a few minutes to be able to move.

She climbed out of the bed, careful not to disturb Boone and Ilias. She used a small bit of her power to complete her plan. A touch to each man's forehead wiped their false memory of drinking until all that was left was the actual events of the past few hours, though she doubted Ilias would be able to sit for the next few days without thinking about what happened. She used another tiny piece of magic to clean herself up and remove all evidence of herself from the room. A quick sidestep through space took her from New York to the sweet-smelling mountains of Colorado. She was full enough that she wouldn't need to return to a populated area for a while. For now, she fully intended to enjoy the solitude and peace that she found in nature. Then, when the time came, she'd seek out another to satisfy her hunger. Maybe a musician the next time around.

## 2 AN APPLE FOR TEACHER

Twenty-four year old Ginn Milton pressed her palms flat against the desk, pushing herself back against the man pounding into her. Trey Ford had come in to discuss his daughter Matilda's spelling grade. After giving Trey a few pointers to help Matilda, Ginn had bent over her desk and flipped up the back of her skirt, exposing the lacy red thong she'd purchased especially for that night. Trey didn't need to be told twice.

He'd wasted no time rolling the proffered condom over his six-inch cock, pulling aside her thong and plunging into Ginn's already-sopping cunt. She felt one of Trey's hands leave her hip and snake around to the front of her panties. As he thrust into her, he slid his fingers past the waistband of her thong and found her clit with practiced ease.

Ginn caught her breath as Trey's finger caressed her nub. She'd gotten lucky – no pun intended – with this one. He stroked her expertly and began adding a swivel to his hips on every other thrust, driving her towards her first orgasm of the night. Neither one of them spoke; only their rapid breathing and the sound of Trey's balls slapping against Ginn's ass could be heard. Ginn made a small whimper as she came, her body shuddering. Trey followed after only a few more thrusts, spilling himself into the condom. He rested for a moment, hands on either side of Ginn's body, before pulling out. He squeezed off the condom and tossed it into the wastebasket next to the desk.

As Ginn straightened, she made a mental note to empty the trash can at the end of the night. It definitely wouldn't do for the janitors to see a bag full of used condoms and wrappers. She smoothed down her skirt, discreetly adjusting her thong. With a wide smile, Ginn turned to Trey. "It was very nice to meet you, Mr. Ford."

"You as well, Ms. Milton," Trey's face was a little flushed, but he looked otherwise unrumpled.

"Give my best to Matilda." Ginn crossed

to the door and opened it. "And please, feel free to come see me again if you ever need anything."

Trey nodded and left the classroom, avoiding eye contact with the parents who were waiting in the chairs just outside the classroom.

"Mr. and Mrs. Black," Ginn's voice was pleasantly professional. "Please, come in." She waited for the couple to pass her before shutting the door. Technically, she didn't need the door closed for this meeting, but it maintained continuity and eliminated suspicion.

After the brief conference, Ginn looked at the next name on her list and smiled. She'd met Rion Andrew on a field trip earlier that year. He was in his early thirties with dark blond hair, chocolate brown eyes and a swimmer's build. He'd been a regular star in her fantasies ever since and she'd hoped he'd be coming to see her.

"Mr. Andrew," Ginn called. Rion stood and followed the teacher into her classroom. She started to speak as the door closed. "Katy is such a joy to have in class."

Less than five minutes later, Ginn was on her knees in front of Rion's chair. She'd unbuttoned her blouse so he could see her breasts straining against the confines of her crimson bra. And then, before he could react with anything more than mild surprise, Ginn had dropped to her knees and reached for his belt buckle.

"What?" Rion managed to stammer as Ginn took him in hand.

She smiled up at him, fingers expertly kneading his gradually hardening flesh. "I like to show my appreciation to single fathers."

Any response Rion had intended to make was lost in an inarticulate growl. Ginn had wrapped her lips around the head of his cock. She teased the slit with the tip of her tongue, letting the salty, musky flavor burst across her taste buds. She kept one hand around the base of his cock, letting more slide into her mouth. As she applied gentle suction to the velvet skin in her mouth, she felt him swell.

Ginn shifted, maneuvering her free hand under her skirt and into her panties. Her clit throbbed as she stroked it and she shivered under her own touch. She let her throat relax and moved her hand from the shaft to his balls. Even as she took Rion's entire length into her mouth and throat, she slipped two fingers into her pussy. She caressed his hot, heavy balls as she ran her tongue up the underside of his dick. She felt his hand on her head as she found a steady rhythm and hoped Rion had enough sense not to force her. The thought fled as soon as it came, more pressing things occupying her mind. Her cunt tightened around her fingers and she knew she was close. One of the things she loved the best about fucking during parent-teacher conferences was that the possibility of being caught turned her on so much that she needed no foreplay.

Her orgasm ran through her entire body, her moans coming out muffled around the cock slipping in and out of her mouth. Her rhythm didn't falter, but began moving faster. Rion's fingers sunk into her hair and she felt his balls tighten in her hand.

"I'm going to cum," Rion managed to gasp out a warning.

Ginn looked up without missing a beat and winked at him. It was the wink that did it. Rion's hips jerked as he came and Ginn pressed her face against him, letting him spurt down her throat. She swallowed, letting the muscles in her throat milk out every last drop. Once she was certain he was done, she let his now limp cock slip from between her lips and sat back on her heels. She rested there for a moment, letting the chemicals in her system dissipate until she was sure she could stand without falling. She leaned back against her desk, buttoning her shirt as Rion tucked himself back into his boxers and zipped up.

"I guess, thank you?" The uncertainty in

Rion's voice made Ginn smile.

"You're welcome." She gave herself a quick once over, running her fingers through her hair and checking her makeup in her compact. She never wore lipstick for obvious reasons. She then glanced at Rion, looking for signs of what they'd done. Other than the flush creeping up his neck, he looked the same.

Ginn walked towards the door, feeling Rion following close behind her. Just before she opened the door, she turned toward him. "This is our little secret, right?"

Rion nodded, still in a bit of a daze. When she opened the door and said good-bye, he gave an automatic response and walked away.

Ginn didn't watch him go. Her gaze had already found her last appointment for the night. Twenty-nine year old Damon Matthews. Medium height, lean, muscled body. Dark brown hair. Pale green eyes. Just enough scruff to make his pretty-boy face drop-dead gorgeous. His son Adam was one of the top pupils in Ginn's class. Adam's older sister Jenna had been equally as gifted.

"Mr. Matthews," Ginn was surprised that her voice had remained even; her stomach was a mass of fluttering heat. "It's good to see you again."

"And you, Miss Milton," Damon said

smoothly as he walked past her.

She'd barely gotten the door shut before Damon grabbed her around the waist and pulled her to him for a scorching kiss. Usually she didn't kiss the men she fucked, but she'd given in last year after Damon made her cum three times during one especially intense 'meeting.' His kiss had almost made her climax again. This one was no different. His mouth devoured hers, lips pressed so hard she knew they'd bruise. When his tongue joined in the assault, she moaned and slid her hands down his back to grab his ass. He pushed her back against the wall, grinding his pelvis against hers so she could feel the hard length of him through the layers of fabric.

Damon nipped at her lips, eliciting surprised yelps as he moved his mouth from hers down her neck. There was a reason she'd put him last on the list. She knew from experience that she'd have little bite marks on her throat, breasts and thighs before the night was through.

Damon's hands were just as busy as his lips. He yanked her blouse out of her skirt and tore the front open. Ginn heard several of the buttons pop off, but couldn't care less as his hands went to her breasts, squeezing and pinching in ways that made juices flood to her already wet pussy. He shoved her skirt up around her waist and then went to work on her thong, all without breaking his mouth's contact with her skin. Ginn tilted her head back and gave herself over to the sensations.

She barely realized that Damon had pushed her panties down to her ankles until he started to move her back to her desk and she had to step out of them. The tiny bit of rational thought she had left hoped that she'd remember to pick them up before she left. Then Damon's lips fastened onto a nipple and she found her concern disappearing. Damon put his hands on her hips and lifted her onto her desk. She made a noise of protest when he released her breast.

"Patience." Damon grinned as he dropped to his knees. "I need a taste first."

Ginn spread her legs immediately and Damon positioned her ass on the very edge of her desk. He ran his tongue around her lips and she moaned. He gave her inner thigh a quick bite, reminding her without words that they needed to be quiet. Out of all of the men she'd fucked over the years, he was the only one who had to remind her not to be loud. When his tongue thrust into her cunt, she remembered why. She stuffed the side of her hand into her mouth, muffling the cry of pleasure that wanted to escape as Damon began to eat her out. He alternated between tongue fucking her and sucking on her clit, never lingering in either place too long. The stubble on his cheeks rubbed the sensitive skin between her legs, adding an element of pain that Ginn found extremely exciting. It didn't take long for her first orgasm to wash over her and she bit down hard enough on her hand to leave marks.

Damon kept his hand on her stomach, preventing her from bucking up against his face as he licked her through her climax. Before she'd completely come down, he had his cock out and a condom on. He stood and positioned himself at her entrance. He waited until her eyes fluttered open before inching his way inside. Rather than the hard, fast fuck the other men gave, Damon paced himself, pushing his dick partway inside, then drawing out and repeating the process. His girth stretched her far more than any of her previous lovers and it rubbed all the right places so that, by the time he finally bottomed out, Ginn was a writhing mess, consumed by the need to cum.

"Damon, just fuck me already," Ginn hissed. She was trying for angry but her words just came out desperate.

He just gave her his infuriating smile, the one that told her he knew exactly what she wanted but that he was going to make her wait for it. He leaned forward, placing his hands on either side of Ginn's waist.

Ginn keened, unable to stop herself. The new position pressed Damon's pelvic bone against her over-stimulated clit.

Damon shook his head and clicked his tongue. "You might want to lower the noise. If we get caught, I hope you know I'm not stopping until I cum."

Ginn stared up at him, unsure if his threat was real. Damon rotated his hips and she bit her bottom lip to keep from calling out. Her hands went to his shoulders and she dug her nails in, marking him even through his shirt. Damon began to thrust in shallow, slow movements, continuing to speak.

"If Mr. Roberts walks in, you know what he'll see? He'll see his third grade teacher, spread on her desk like a whore, getting fucked so hard that she won't be able to walk straight for a week." Damon's voice was surprisingly even. "I bet you'd like that, wouldn't you? You'd like to see the look on his face as I pound into you. Watch his eyes widen behind those little wire-rim glasses as he sees those pretty tits of yours bouncing with every thrust."

To emphasize his point, Damon pulled further out, his inward stroke more forceful than before. Ginn moaned.

"I bet he'd even keep you around afterwards, so at teachers' meetings, he could stare at you, picturing you naked, breasts jiggling, as a cock rams into your tight little cunt," Damon dropped down so his mouth was right next to Ginn's ear. "Maybe he'll even ask me to come in and fuck you in front of the entire faculty."

Ginn's back arched, mouth opening in a silent scream as electricity ran through her entire body. Her toes curled, muscles clenched as she climaxed. Damon didn't miss a stroke, forcing his dick through the spasming walls of Ginn's cunt and triggering another orgasm. Her vision went white and she was only vaguely aware that Damon was now pounding into her even harder, grunting with the effort. She knew she'd be sore as soon as the endorphins wore off, but couldn't bring herself to care. All she wanted now was to keep riding this wave of pleasure and Damon was doing just that.

"Fuck," Damon cursed as he came hard, collapsing on top of Ginn as his cock pulsed inside her, filling the condom with his cum. Damon buried his face against Ginn's neck, muscles twitching and trembling from the force of his climax. It was almost a full minute before either one of them could move.

Ginn moaned as Damon pulled out, feeling the warmth of her own juices running down her legs. She propped herself up on her elbows as Damon slumped in her chair. He tossed the condom into the waste can and then looked up at her.

"I'm thinking we might need to meet again soon to discuss Adam's progress." One side of Damon's mouth quirked up in a half-smile. "These bi-annual conferences don't really do the trick."

Ginn nodded, eyes sparkling. "I agree. I'm thinking more frequent meetings might be in order."

"So, next week, same time?" Damon stood, straightening his clothes.

"I'll make sure it's on my calendar," Ginn promised.

Damon winked at her as he exited the classroom. Ginn let herself fall back against her desk. Damn, she loved her job.

# 3 HOUSE OF SHADOWS

The house was dark when Ranie returned, but she knew that her companions inside were watching, waiting for her. She set the bag of groceries on the porch, pushed her short black curls out of her face and stepped inside. She hadn't gone more than a few feet down the darkened hallway before a pair of strong arms wrapped around her, one hand covering her mouth, and she was thrown against the wall. She brought up a knee, but it was blocked. She grabbed at the shirt of the man holding her and fisted the material, tugging on it. One of his hands slid underneath the hem of her shirt, bare palm skimming over her flat stomach.

She laughed; she couldn't help it. The

hand over her mouth fell away. "It tickles," she protested. Her gray eyes danced.

The blond man in front of her didn't look quite as amused. Ranie grabbed the back of Zak's neck and pulled his head down so their lips could meet. Her tongue traced his bottom lip and he opened his mouth. Her tongue slid along his as she pressed her body flush against his, the hard length of him firm against her stomach.

"Get a room," Ranie's younger sister, Cyndee, complained as she passed through the hallway to retrieve the bag from the porch. "Tym and I are fine on watch."

Ranie grinned up at Zak, grabbed his hand and pulled him up the stairs. Cyndee rolled her blue-gray eyes and took the supplies into the kitchen. She was two years younger than Ranie and the youngest on the team. Tym and Ranie were twenty and Zak was twenty-three. He'd been moved up to rank one with Ranie as his second. Cyndee and Tym rounded out the top four. Cyndee pulled her thick mahogany hair back from her face and tied it up behind her head. She and Ranie were the only two siblings to be a part of the Shadow Project and she knew it was in large part to Ranie having refused to leave her little sister behind when the recruiters came. Cyndee had been only fourteen, the youngest member of the Project, and had to fight to prove that she had a right to stay. This mission was her chance to show, once and for all, that Ranie hadn't been the only reason she'd made it to the final twelve.

Upstairs, the assignment was the furthest thing from Ranie and Zak's minds. They'd been paired off for years, but this mission was the first opportunity they'd had to be together outside of the Project. The door had barely shut behind them before they began divesting themselves of their clothing. They'd been given civilian clothing for the mission, but nothing was fancy. Still, Zak's dark green eyes glowed with an almost predatory light at the sight of Ranie in her white cotton bra and panties. His hands were on her before she could take either off, pulling her to him until their skin – bare for all but their underwear – touched.

"I've been waiting a long time to do this," Zak whispered in Ranie's ear as he ran his hands up her arms and around to her back. His breath was hot against her neck.

"You've been fucking me for two years, Zak," Ranie retorted, raking her nails lightly down his back. She smiled at his sharp intake of air.

Zak retaliated by scraping his teeth over her earlobe, enjoying the feel of her shivering against him. "None of that is even close to what I'm going to do with you tonight." His fingers skillfully unhooked her bra and she shrugged out of it.

"Really?" Ranie was intrigued. Zak was the tough one, the epitome of the strong, silent type. Their sex had rarely included talking of any kind.

Zak hooked his fingers into the waistband of her panties. He pressed his lips against her throat, moving up to her chin and then her mouth. He covered her lips with his, tongue seeking entrance as he pushed her backwards towards the wall. Their tongues dueled for dominance, neither one wanting to give an inch. When Zak finally pulled back, both were panting. He dropped to his knees, sliding Ranie's panties down her long, athletic legs. She stepped out of them.

"No curfews. No superiors doing surprise inspections," Zak tossed the underwear aside and looked up at Ranie. "No paper thin walls with ten others and who knows how many guards listening."

"Cyndee and Tym," Ranie started to say.

Zak interrupted her. "Are only two and are downstairs. They might hear us." A wicked grin spread across his face and Ranie felt herself grow wet at the promise in that smile. "In fact, I'm betting they will since I plan on making you scream."

Ranie raised an eyebrow. "Promises,

promises."

Zak didn't reply, instead wrapping a hand around the back of one of Ranie's knees. He hooked her leg over his shoulder and buried his face between her legs. Zak ate pussy like he did everything else: whole-heartedly and with grim determination. His tongue danced across her skin, starting at the sensitive inside of her thighs and passing over her lips, circling but not quite touching where she most wanted him. When he dipped into her core, Ranie's head fell back against the wall with a thump. She dropped a hand to Zak's head, fingers twining in his hair.

"Please," she pleaded as he began to thrust his tongue into her cunt the same way he'd done to her mouth. She tried to push him against her, to move him where she wanted him to go. A quick turn of his head and a nip to her inner thigh made her yelp. She kept her hand on his head but relinquished control. Zak rewarded her by flicking his tongue across her clit and she cried out.

Cyndee and Tym sat in the living room, positioned in front of the large picture window that gave them a clear view of their target's home. Neither one spoke as they both tried to ignore the sounds from upstairs. In their haste, Zak and Ranie had chosen the room with the air vent that lead directly to the living room. Cyndee kept her binoculars trained on the house despite the fact that it was well after midnight and the last light in the house had gone off over an hour before.

Tym ran a hand through his thick brown hair, shifting uncomfortably in his seat. The Shadow Project never minded the agents using each other for stress relief, as long as no emotional connection was made, but it had been a few weeks since Tym had had an opportunity to hook up with one of the six female agents. Well, five since Ranie and Zak didn't do anyone but each other. And, technically, Tym had only been with four of the others. Cyndee hadn't turned eighteen until just a few months ago and none of the men wanted to risk bodily harm by trying to fuck Ranie's little sister. Even if Cyndee didn't break their nose or bust their balls for just asking, Ranie certainly would. Problem was, now they were in close quarters with what could've passed for a porn soundtrack coming from upstairs and Tym was getting hard.

Cyndee squirmed, unable to concentrate on anything other than the dampness between her legs. She hadn't technically been a virgin since before she and Ranie joined the Project, but a few quickies with a boyfriend in the backseat of his car didn't really count for much experience. Then she'd spent the last four years around physically fit and, for the most part, totally gorgeous men who couldn't look at her because of her age and then wouldn't look at her because of her sister. She'd had her share of crushes among the six male agents, but in the past year, she'd really only been thinking about one. It had been Tym's warm brown eyes she'd picture late at night in her bunk, hand between her legs. It was his face she imagined above her, his cock she'd wanted in place of her fingers. And now, with her sister crying out above, Cyndee was about ready to explode.

"Fuck it," she muttered.

"What?" Tym looked at her startled. The astonishment on his face increased as Cyndee stood, grabbed the hem of her shirt and pulled it over her head. His jaw dropped when she yanked off her jeans. She was thinner than most of the recruits, almost frail-looking, but he thought he'd never seen anything so beautiful.

"If you're too noble, or whatever, to make a move, then I'll do it," Cyndee took the steps needed until she stood directly in front of him. "I want you. I've wanted you for a while."

"But... I..." Tym stammered.

Cyndee reached behind her and unhooked her bra, letting it slip off her arms. Her breasts were small, tipped by light brown nipples that hardened in the cool night air. She quickly stepped out of her panties, revealing that she was, indeed, a natural redhead. "I'm not a virgin, Tym, if that's what you're worried about."

Tym gaped at her, hand involuntarily dropping to his crotch in an attempt to make his erection less obvious.

Cyndee sighed. "I see I'm going to have to do all the work." She grinned and leaned down to slant her mouth over Tym's, forcing his lips open with her tongue. He was tall enough that she didn't have to bend far. He groaned into her mouth as his resolve melted away. He cupped one breast in his hand as he used his other hand to bury his fingers in the hair at the nape of her neck. She ran a hand down his muscular chest down to his crotch. She smiled against his mouth as his dick swelled beneath her touch. The hand on her breast slid down her side to her hip, fingers digging in as she manipulated the button and zipper on Tym's pants.

Tym pulled back, breaking the kiss long enough to tug his pants and boxers down enough to free his aching member. When

Cyndee wrapped a hand around his shaft, Tym's head fell back, eyelids fluttering. She stroked him a few times, reveling in the feel of velvet-covered steel, the heavy heat of him. He was much larger than her boyfriend had been. She placed a leg on either side of his hips, for the first time thanking the higher ups at the Project who had made pregnancy impossible. Combine that with routine testing and physicals and Cyndee knew that she could do this without risk. When she removed her hand, Tym opened his eyes, pupils blown so wide that only a thin sliver of brown could be seen around a circle of black. Their gazes locked as she began to lower herself onto him.

"Shit," Tym swore under his breath as his crown made its way into her moist warmth. Her walls clenched almost too much as she forced him inside her. Even through the pleasure, he searched her face for any indication of pain. She may not have been a virgin, but she was as tight as one. His hands fisted at his sides, the muscles in his neck standing out as he fought for control.

"Almost there," Cyndee breathed, the pleasure-pain of him stretching her making her words little more than air. She gasped as his cock brushed against a spot inside her, knees buckling. She dropped the remaining inches, grunting in surprise as she suddenly found herself resting on Tym's lap. She rested her forehead against his chest for a moment, letting her adapt to the feeling of fullness.

"Cyndee," Tym pleaded, sliding his hands up her slim legs to her hips. "Please."

Cyndee grabbed the bottom of his T-shirt and yanked it over his head. She moved her hips, just a bit, just enough to make Tym swear again, and smiled. She lowered her mouth to his chest, sucking the skin into her mouth, tasting the salt on his skin as she began to raise herself an inch or two before pushing back down again.

"Fuck, fuck, fuck, fuck," Ranie dug her nails into Zak's shoulders as he pushed himself inside her in one smooth stroke.

"That's the idea," he panted. He didn't pause, didn't wait to see if she was ready, just drew himself out of her and slammed back in, drawing a breathless keen from her kiss-swollen lips.

Ranie hooked her leg around his waist, her other foot barely touching the ground as each thrust lifted her off her feet. She could feel every splinter jabbing into her back, could feel the bruises starting to form on her hips where Zak held her, but she only cried out for more, wanting him to move harder, faster, knowing she would feel him inside her for days. Every cell in her body hummed with pain-laced pleasure as Zak pounded into her. She'd already cum twice, once from his mouth, once from his fingers, and she could feel the third building.

Zak nipped at her throat, tongue laving over where his teeth had stung. He knew she had to be close; he'd been her lover for over two years and knew her responses almost as well as she did. His mouth reached the place where her neck and shoulder met. He bit down hard enough to leave an impression, and Ranie's cunt convulsed around his cock. She called out his name as she climaxed, clinging to him to keep her from crumpling to the floor. He didn't stop, relentlessly fucking her through her orgasm and into another.

It was almost too much. Her skin felt like it was on fire, the very air caressing her glistening body made her nerves sing. She couldn't move, couldn't do anything but hold onto Zak's shoulders as his hips snapped forward again and again, driving his cock deeper and deeper inside until she wasn't sure where one of them ended and the other began. Then his mouth was against his ear and his words made her whimper.

"You're going to scream for me. Scream so loud, Cyndee and Tym will think of it every time they look at you. I want your throat raw, your voice hoarse." Zak felt his balls drawing up and knew his own climax was close.

Ranie nodded mutely, unable to speak as wave after wave of pleasure washed over her. Then, without warning, Zak dropped to his knees, his dick withdrawing almost completely as Ranie followed him. He raised his hips to meet her, the combination of gravity and his upward motion plunging him further inside than he'd ever been before and Ranie did indeed scream. Her entire body shook as Zak emptied himself into her, her orgasm triggering his own.

"Way to go Zak," Tym couldn't resist a comment even as he thrust up into Cyndee's lithe body. She leaned back, baring her breasts to his mouth.

"Let's see if we can give them a run for their money," Cyndee gasped, gyrating her pelvis in a way that made Tym growl around her nipple.

"You asked for it," he warned. In one swift movement, he stood, taking Cyndee with him. He dropped her on the table and hooked her ankles around her neck. Every thrust made her pert little breasts jiggle and he reached for them, rolling her nipples between his fingers until she squirmed underneath him.

"Harder," Cyndee gasped. "I'm not fucking glass."

Tym grinned and increased his pace, his balls slapping against her ass as he pounded into her. He shifted his hips and she wailed.

"There, again, there!" Her fingers scrabbled against the tabletop.

Her partner was only too eager to comply and repeated the motion. Her cunt squeezed his cock and he swore. He wasn't going to last much longer. She was too tight and it had been too long. He dropped one hand from her breast and pressed it against her clit, forcing her from one orgasm into the next.

"Shit, yes, please," Cyndee raised her hips to meet his, the pleasure almost too intense. "Fuck!" She drew out the word in one long cry as she felt Tym explode inside her.

Upstairs, Ranie raised her head from Zak's chest and grinned. "Sounds like Cyndee finally got her man."

"It's about time." Zak wrapped his arms around Ranie as their heart rates dropped back down to normal.

"Think we'll actually be able to get some

work done now?"

Zak brushed sweat-dampened curls from Ranie's forehead. "I'm sure the four of us will be able to work out a feasible schedule. We may even let the Project know that long-term surveillance might be needed."

Ranie traced her fingers over Zak's chest. "Sounds good to me. I like where I am right now."

"Me, too." He pressed his lips against the top of Ranie's head. "But, I think for now, we need to get some sleep. For some reason, I'm really tired."

Ranie chuckled and closed her eyes, letting sleep take her. Zak was close behind, his body curled protectively around his second in command. Downstairs, Cyndee and Tym were retrieving their clothes, now relaxed enough to continue their watch without further interruption. Well, maybe not a lot of interruptions.

# 4 LATE FEES

His hands were on her, cupping her breasts as his lips teased her nipples into hard points. She arched her back, pushing her breasts towards his talented mouth. She parted her knees, hooking her ankles around his hips to pull him towards her. She knew what she wanted... .

"Excuse me, miss?"

Twenty-four year-old Aubrey Madison blinked, pulling herself from her reverie. The young man in front of her was looking at her expectantly. "Sorry," she said, smiling.

"No problem." He slid two books across the counter. "Must get boring doing the night shift at a college library, especially up here on the second floor."

Aubrey didn't answer as she scanned the books. A glint had come into the young man's eyes and she knew what would be coming next. Any time an upperclassman came into the library late at night and saw her, they immediately decided she must be lonely and in the need of male companionship. Aubrey wasn't stupid. She knew she was pretty. Golden blond curls that hung just past her shoulders. Fair and lightly freckled skin. Tall with just enough curves on an athletic build and, of course her most startling feature, long-lashed light violet eyes. Thing was, she wasn't looking for a relationship, especially from some college student with no idea where he was going or what he wanted to do with his life.

"I don't mind." Aubrey tried to keep her voice polite without encouraging him. She pushed the books back across the counter. "Have a good night."

With a disappointed glance over his shoulder, the young man walked away. Aubrey watched him go, scanning around her to determine if anyone was nearby or if she could go back to her little fantasy. A noise to her right caught her attention. Aubrey sighed. Freshman liked to use the second floor for trysts and she hated having to be the one to kick them out. There was the embarrassed stammering, the tugging at clothes, and more skin than she generally wanted to see. One couple hadn't wanted to leave, enjoying the fact that Aubrey had been standing there. It had taken the threat of campus police to finally get them out. Now, Aubrey headed back towards the secluded, shadowed area at the back of the second floor, the noises growing louder the closer she got. She didn't try to sneak as she made her way through the stacks. She'd hoped the sound of her approaching feet would stop the couple before she arrived, but no such luck. As she rounded the corner, she opened her mouth to speak, and found the words caught in her throat.

The slim coed on the floor had long, dark hair fanned out across the pale gray tile. Her eyes were closed, head tilted back to reveal a young, pale face. Her blouse was open, bra pushed up to expose small, pert breasts. Her skirt was bunched around her waist, allowing the man between her legs easy access. He wore an expensive suit and hadn't bothered actually removing any clothing. His hips were pumping furiously, his grunts echoing in the still air. But it was the back of his neck that had captured Aubrey's attention. She'd seen pictures of that birthmark before. In fact, Senator Alden Kain's recent presidential bid had made the wine-colored splotch widely known. Aubrey had a moment to wonder what the conservative family man's constituents would think if they could hear him, punctuating his gasps with random obscenities as he thrust into the young woman beneath him. The girl seemed to be enjoying herself, murmuring encouragement as she raised her hips to meet his. Her hands clung to his shoulders as the senator's pace increased. He came with a groan and rested for only a second before rolling off of his partner.

Aubrey slipped behind one of the shelves, suddenly curious about the clandestine meeting.

"Are you going to tell her?" The girl's voice was soft, but still sounded loud in the library hush.

The senator sat up, dark hair damp with sweat. He was younger than Aubrey had first thought, closer to late thirties than mid-forties. He didn't answer the girl as he tucked himself back into his pants. She rolled on her side and repeated her question, this time with a bit more force. Aubrey felt her curiosity turn to horror as Senator Kain's hands closed around the girl's neck.

"Sorry, darling," the senator said in a low voice.

Aubrey stumbled backwards, unable to stop herself. She knew she'd made noise and that the senator might have seen her, but none of that mattered now. All she cared about was getting away.

When the assignment was announced, twenty-five year-old Gray Gibson immediately accepted the job for protective duty. A few of the rookies gave him a puzzled look, but those who'd known him over the past few years understood. Gray had never lacked for female attention. He was tall, muscular, with light brown hair and bright green eyes. His features weren't quite delicate enough for him to be pretty, but a bit more so than he needed to be considered ruggedly handsome. In addition to his physical attractiveness, Gray was exactly the right type of man to take home to the parents. Unfortunately, he always seemed to be unlucky in love.

"You want to take primary on this, Gibson?" The captain had been Gray's mentor and was still the young man's confidant. When Gray's girlfriend of five years ran off to Vegas with her yoga instructor shortly after Gray's proposal, it had been Captain Miller that Gray had turned to. For the past six months, Gray had been throwing himself into the job, convinced that it would fill the void Samantha had left behind. Captain Miller disagreed but, unlike some of Gray's other friends, hadn't tried setting him up on dates. This, however, was different. Captain Miller had met Aubrey Madison the night before and instantly knew that she'd be perfect for Gray. Now, if only he could get Gray to see it too.

Aubrey stretched out on the bed and sighed. She'd been confined to the hotel room for four days and cabin fever was setting in. She glanced over at the other bed, already knowing what – or who – she'd see. Gray Gibson was definitely one of the better-looking men she'd seen and there was just something about the way he spoke that made her insides heat up. She was far from the type of person who fell for someone after just a few days. In fact, she generally mocked those who did the whole 'love at first sight' thing. Granted, when most people said that they'd spent four days together, it wasn't for all twenty-four hours of each day, but she still knew this reaction was unusual for her. Her fantasies were always about fictional characters; she never daydreamed about the men she knew.

Gray, on the other hand, had always been a hopeless romantic, prone to falling head over heels, usually with the worst possible person. When he'd first met Aubrey, he'd been struck first by her sweet spirit and then by her beauty. Captain Miller's knowing look when handing over the case file had made immediate sense.

He'd balked at the idea of a set-up, but still found himself making excuses to send his relief home so he could stay. Then, that morning, he'd found himself staring at Aubrey's sleeping figure on the next bed. The innocent expression on her face stirred a desire to protect her that went far deeper than what was required by his badge. When she'd woken, he'd busied himself looking elsewhere, anywhere but at her. Over the past few days, both had been comfortable with the silence that reigned most of the time, but today was different. There was a heat and tension in the room that became almost palpable as afternoon turned into evening.

As the evening began, it became obvious to Aubrey that Gray wasn't going to act on what they were both obviously feeling. She knew the risk of what she was considering, but after having been celibate for too long and then spending days cooped up with a gorgeous man who smelled as good as he looked, her decision was easy enough.

"I'm going to take a shower," Aubrey announced. Out of the corner of her eye, she saw Gray nod absently. Time to up the stakes. She started towards the bathroom, yanking off her shirt before she got inside. Her black satin bra was far from fancy, but she knew it showed off her curves. Pausing just outside the doorway, she slid off her pants and kicked them aside, being sure to give Gray a full view of her firm ass. She left the door partway open, tossing her bra and panties back into the room where she knew Gray could see them.

Gray swore under his breath as the underwear dropped to the floor. He couldn't see into the bathroom from where he sat on the bed, but just knowing Aubrey was naked was enough to get him hard. He'd refrained from jerking off in the shower for the past four days, concerned both that Aubrey might hear him and that he might take too long and something would happen. He hadn't had sex in months, but at least when he'd been at home, he'd gotten some kind of relief. He dropped his hand to his crotch, pressing his heel against his erection and trying to will it away.

Aubrey let the warm spray cascade over her as a plan formed in her mind. With a sigh, she ran her hands over her soapy skin, giving herself over to the sensations. When she cupped her breasts, fingers playing across her hardening nipples, she felt a rush of warmth in her belly. She moaned, making no effort to quiet herself. She wanted Gray to know exactly what she was doing.

At the sound coming from the bathroom, Gray's cock swelled from half to full mast. He bit back a groan as Aubrey began to punctuate her moans with words.

She slid her hand between her legs, her index finger easily slipping into her cunt. "Fuck, yes." Her thumb brushed her clit and she shuddered. Time to up the ante. "Yes, Gray, fuck! Yes!"

Gray started when he heard his name, thinking it must've been a mistake. Then, he heard her call out his name again.

"Please, fuck me, Gray!"

He didn't give himself the chance to think, knowing he'd second guess himself if he did. He jumped out of the bed, tugging off his clothes as he went.

Aubrey heard Gray enter, not quite as preoccupied as she sounded. When she could see his shadow on the curtain, she spoke, this time directly to Gray. "Care to give me a hand?" When Gray pulled aside the curtain, Aubrey grinned and amended, "or you could give me something else."

Gray didn't respond. He climbed into the shower, gaze never leaving Aubrey's wet, glistening body. Her chest and neck were flushed with arousal, her nipples hard and pointed. The fine curls between her legs revealed her to be a natural blond.

Likewise, Aubrey let her eyes roam over Gray's body. His clothes had been well-made enough for her to suspect what they covered, but her imagination hadn't done him justice. Gray was a few inches taller than Aubrey, with wide shoulders and a torso muscled from hours at the gym. His abs were sculpted under tan skin and a trail of dark hair ran from his belly button down to the hard length of him that rose up, swollen and ready.

Aubrey didn't say another word, just reached down, wrapping her hand around the hot, heavy shaft. Gray made a low sound and pulled Aubrey to him. Her lips opened under his, tongues teasing each other with shallow, rapid thrusts. Skin slid against skin as Gray tightened his grip, his leaking cock rubbing against Aubrey's stomach.

Gray used his teeth to tug on Aubrey's bottom lip and she writhed against him, nails biting into Gray's muscular ass. Aubrey tilted her head back, giving Gray's mouth access to her throat.

"I need you inside me now," Aubrey's voice was breathless.

"The bed," Gray tried to protest.

"We can make love later," Aubrey backed up until her back was against the cool tile wall. "Right now, I just want you in me."

"I am here to serve," Gray quipped. His words were humorous but the look in his eyes was anything but. Aubrey spread her legs in a blatant invitation and anything else Gray had considered saying dried up in his mouth. He took a single step, grabbed Aubrey's thigh in his hand, lifting it enough for him to bury himself in Aubrey's pussy in one swift thrust. Aubrey cried out as he filled her, the muscles in her cunt spasming as they adjusted to Gray's size. Gray pressed his face against Aubrey's throat, swearing at the sensation of being sheathed in her wet heat.

"Come on, Gray," Aubrey whispered into his ear. "Fuck me until I can't remember my name."

Gray didn't speak but his actions said it all. He dragged himself slowly out of Aubrey's pussy until just the head remained. She whimpered at the loss, wiggling her hips in an attempt to get him back inside. Gray pressed back inside, letting his dick feel every smooth, silken inch until he bottomed out. Aubrey's nails scratched at his back as he repeated the movement, never moving any faster.

"Please," Aubrey nearly sobbed. Her body felt like it was on fire, like every drop of water that touched her should sizzle. With everything that had happened in the past week, she needed to cum and Gray's slow, deep thrusts were keeping her just on the edge without letting her tumble over.

Gray's tongue darted out, licking the water and sweat from Aubrey's skin. The faint taste of her body wash lingered on his tongue. The sting from his savaged back pushed him to the line between pain and pleasure and he felt himself losing control. His hips snapped forward, eliciting a high, keening note from Aubrey. The sound spurred him forward and he began to pound into her, the strength of his thrusts lifting her almost off of her feet. He felt her orgasm as the muscles in her body stiffened and she swore. He followed her after just two more strokes, crying out her name as he emptied himself into her. His knees shook and he gently lowered them both into the tub before withdrawing. He wrapped his arms around Aubrey, cradling her against his chest.

She winked at him. "Now I'm thinking your bed suggestion is a good idea."

With a gentle laugh, Gray stood and held out a hand. Aubrey took it and let him lead her to the bed they'd be sharing for the remainder of their stay.

Gray lifted her up, bridal style, and laid her down on the bed with a gentleness that made Aubrey sigh blissfully. Here in the bedroom, she could see Gray's every muscle rippling underneath her hand. His washboard abs made her mouth water and so did his hard cock that was standing proudly. Aubrey felt herself getting wetter and bit the inside of her cheek in anticipation.

Gray could only stare at Aubrey's naked body beneath him. Her breasts were firm and perky; her nipples hard. She had a tiny waist that led to her hips and all the way down to her long, slim legs. The moonlight made her skin glow. She looked ethereal, like she was just a dream that would disappear if he wasn't careful. She was perfect.

They kissed passionately, tongues intertwining, skin against skin. It was almost painful not to be inside her, his cock missing the heat that it experienced before. He let his hands wander, exploring Aubrey's body, finding every dip of her curves. He moved lower, leaving a trail of heat in his wake with long licks and kisses, making Aubrey moan and writhe beneath him. He gave Aubrey's pussy one long lick, stopping at the little nub.

Aubrey couldn't believe how talented Gray was with his tongue. His ministrations felt amazing as electricity coursed throughout her body. But no matter how pleasurable it felt, she was impatient to have him inside her. "Please," she said, rubbing his cheek with her hand.

Gray didn't need to be told twice. He

lifted Aubrey's legs and put the back of her knees on top of his shoulders as he positioned himself at her entrance. He thrust inside her with one quick motion, making Aubrey arch her back. Gray was surprised at how wet Aubrey had become. He could feel her juices dripping on the bed and her scent wafted through his nose, making him want her more. It was hard, having to control himself, but he didn't want to hurt her because of his impatience. It was only when he felt nails scrape his back encouragingly that he started moving. He didn't even bother starting out slow; instead he pumped inside her as fast as he could. He reveled in her heat and wetness, amazed at how perfectly they fit together. It was as if their bodies were made for each other.

Aubrey came first, spasming and screaming Gray's name. He came after five more thrusts, his whole body tensing. But he was still hard, and Aubrey still wanted more. He laid down on the bed, bringing Aubrey on top of him. She didn't need to be told what to do; she knew what he wanted.

She positioned herself on top of his cock and took him in slowly, inch by inch. He was in so deep that Aubrey could do nothing but bite her lower lip. She took Gray's hands and put them on her hips. The way Gray was staring at her body was making her hornier and she wanted to give Gray a show.

Gray moaned at the sight of Aubrey moving her hips. It was as if she was dancing to a non-existent beat and it did wonders to his cock. She put her hands above her head, giving Gray a delicious view of her lithe body. When he couldn't take it anymore, he sat up, pulling Aubrey close to him. He took the lead, letting Aubrey bounce up and down on his length. He knew the exact moment she was going to come when he felt her pussy squeeze him at the last second before she moaned loudly, her body spasming again. As they lay back onto the bed, he let her rest for a few minutes.

Rousing herself, Aubrey took him in her mouth, her head bobbing up and down. She let her tongue roam all over his cock, tasting her own juices in the process.

Not wanting to be rough, Gray put his hands behind his back to stop himself from holding Aubrey's head still so he could fuck her mouth. He was close, he could feel the pressure building and building and before he knew it, he came violently in her mouth.

She looked up at him and swallowed the hot liquid and then licked the corners of her mouth. Aubrey smiled at him and laid beside him, curling into his side.

"Gray?" Aubrey said as she pressed her

cheek against his bare skin. "What happens if someone comes after me?"

Gray pressed his lips to the top of Audrey's head. "I won't let them touch you."

Aubrey looked up, a smile starting to form. "And me?"

Gray's eyes lit up with emotion. "I'll let you touch me."

Aubrey chuckled. "I'll hold you to that."

"I'll keep you safe, Aubrey," Gray brushed back her wet curls. "And when this is all over..." His voice trailed off.

"I'll want you then, too." Aubrey pushed herself up so that her lips brushed against Gray's.

He grinned and pressed a kiss onto the tip of her nose. "Sounds like a plan."

# 5 WILD PLACES

The Whaley House had been one of Cici's favorites. Not because she and Davis had seen any ghosts, mind you. When they'd arrived at the house to find it open to the public and filled with the typical, paranormal crowd, they'd immediately dismissed the reports of haunting as marketing. Still, it hadn't meant that they could leave without investigating further.

They both took their job seriously, but neither one was about to pass up an opportunity for a little fun. Once they'd satisfied their suspicions and found the place clear of any supernatural activity, they'd ducked into a side room.

The closet hadn't been very big, but it was enough for what they wanted. Cici wasted no time shimmying her shorts and underwear down to her knees. Davis unzipped his shorts, pulling out his already-hard cock. The excitement of the possible hunt, the thrill of knowing they might be caught, all had Cici wet and ready. Davis didn't bother with any preliminaries. He and Cici had been lovers since she was sixteen and he knew her body as well as his own. When he slid inside, Cici made a muffled noise and David grinned. She was usually such a vocal lover that having to be quiet was pure torture.

Davis wrapped one arm around Cici's waist, hand perfectly positioned for rubbing her clit. His other hand slipped under her T-shirt and bra, cupping one full breast. The small space didn't allow for much maneuvering so Davis kept his thrusts shallow. He curved himself over Cici's back, mouth sucking at the skin at the back of her neck as he worked her clit in time with his strokes.

"Davis," Cici whimpered. Her body felt like it was on fire as it hovered just on the brink of orgasm.

Davis moved his lips to Cici's ear. "Shh," he rotated his hips and Cici turned her face into her arm. "Wouldn't want anyone to come investigate strange noises, now would we?" The muscles around his cock twitched and he smiled, a wicked light coming into his dark gray eyes. "Or would you? That's it, isn't it? You'd love for someone to catch us, wouldn't you? Some stranger opening the door to see you getting fucked wide open by my cock, tits half out of your bra, panting like some bitch in heat while I rub your clit."

Cici sank her teeth into the flesh of her upper arm as her body started to quiver. Her boyfriend knew exactly what to say to get her ready to cum. Davis gave one final thrust, emptying himself into his girlfriend. "Now," he commanded.

The order, combined with the feeling of Davis spurting inside her, shoved Cici over the edge and she shook with the force of her orgasm and the struggle to swallow her screams.

When the couple emerged from the closet a minute later, only the slight muss to Cici's short, white blond hair indicated that they'd been doing something naughty. And since everyone on the tour was more interested in the possibility of ghosts than the idea of a sexual tryst, no one noticed anything out of the ordinary.

Nineteen year old Cici Rose and her twenty-one year old boyfriend Davis Forester had been hunting ghosts together for six years. Cici's parents had raised her in the life, never staying in one place long, never making any friends. Then, when she was thirteen, she and her parents found a fifteen year-old survivor of a mysterious attack. Davis had joined the Rose family in their quest to confront the supernatural. Four years later, her parents disappeared while on a hunt. From that point on, she and Davis had continued on alone, all the while searching for clues about what had happened to their respective parents, and if Cici's were still alive.

They were halfway to their next destination when the storm hit. Cici's sharp blue-green eyes had spotted the hotel sign before Davis and she pointed it out. The Lightning Post was a sprawling, three story inn with a classic, rustic look. As they pulled into the gravel parking lot, the pair exchanged glances. It was deserted. Not a single vehicle and no lights in any of the windows, not even a porch light.

"What do you think?" Davis ran a hand through his dark brown hair.

"I'm thinking I don't want to spend the night in the car," Cici replied. "You have your kit?"

Davis patted his jacket pocket.

"Then let's go."

They dashed for the doors, soaked to the skin even in the few feet they had to cross. The overhang provided enough cover for Davis - after trying the door and finding it locked - to take out his lock picks and quickly work the mechanics so the door clicked open. Based on the lack of visibility and the remoteness of the area, they were fairly confident that no one would bother them.

Once inside, they paused to look around. The lobby was small, containing only a dusty desk and a few creaky wooden chairs. The only light came from a single flickering lamp that looked like it was on its way out.

"Light?" Cici pitched her voice low, but it still echoed.

Davis nodded, retrieving a flashlight from the pocket of his jacket while Cici pulled one from her shoulder bag. Neither one had grabbed any of their actual luggage, but Cici kept her bag with her at all times. Davis never commented on it. He didn't have to. He knew that, tucked in an inside pocket was the only picture Cici had left of her parents. Everything else had disappeared with Mr. and Mrs. Rose. All they'd had left was the bag Cici had taken with her when they'd left for the movies that night.

As they began their canvas of the first floor, Davis kept his free hand at his back, fingers wrapped around the grip of his Colt. He knew, without having to look, that Cici had her knife at hand. They hadn't lasted as long as they had by being reckless. After finishing with the first floor – consisting of an old-fashioned kitchen, quaint dining room and parlor – they moved upstairs. While on the second floor, the couple found the reason for the hotel's desertion. Cici held up the newspaper for Davis to read the headline. "Lightning Post to Close after Mysterious Deaths." Once satisfied that they were indeed alone, they returned to the first floor. It was close to midnight by the time they finished and they both knew that they wouldn't be going anywhere else that night.

Cici shivered. The room by room search had kept her mind off of her wet clothes, but now she was starting to feel the chill. Remembering that the parlor had a fireplace, she took Davis's hand and led him into the tiny room. It was barely eight feet squared, with an antique-looking sofa perfectly positioned in front of the massive fireplace that took up nearly the entire far wall. Directly next to it was a bin of wood.

It didn't take much to get a fire going. Cici stood in front of it, sighing as the warmth washed over her. She closed her eyes, concentrating on the heat rather than the clammy feel of her wet clothing. Then she felt Davis's hands on her shoulders and she opened her eyes, turning towards her boyfriend.

"Let's get out of these wet things," Davis's words and tone were innocent enough, but Cici felt a bolt of desire shoot straight through her.

"Sounds like a great idea," Cici replied, voice low and sultry. The heat in her eyes was enough to make Davis's blood surge south. Cici's next words brought him to half-mast. "What do you say we warm each other up a bit?" Cici pulled off her shirt, the wet cloth sliding across her slick skin. Her simple cotton bra was white, now transparent. Her caramel-colored nipples were hard points beneath the cold fabric. By the time she divested herself of her jeans, Davis's own clothes were laid out in front of the fire, his impressive shaft curving up towards his stomach.

"Might as well let them dry," he shrugged, taking a few extra seconds to stretch Cici's clothing flat.

When he turned back around, he found Cici on the couch, legs spread in a blatant invitation. Cici smiled up at her boyfriend as she ran her finger down between her now bare breasts and between her folds.

Davis took two steps and dropped to his knees between Cici's legs. She leaned forward, lips pressing against his, tongue penetrating his mouth. Davis cupped the back of Cici's head, deepening the kiss so that their tongues dueled for dominance.

Cici finally pulled back, whispering

against Davis's lips, "I want that mouth on my pussy."

"Always happy to oblige," Davis wasted no time burying his face between Cici's thighs.

Cici fell back against the sofa as Davis dipped his tongue into her dripping cunt. The thick muscle worked inside her, teasing her silken walls, dancing back out to dart up and around her clit.

"Shit," Cici's head fell back as her body sang with pleasure. Across the ceiling, a strange shadow flitted by. Cici's eyes tracked it for a moment before Davis's talented mouth distracted her again.

Davis dropped a hand to his erection, hot and heavy with need. He stroked himself slowly as Cici exploded around his tongue, her natural exquisite flavor mingling with the taste of the rain as it exploded across his taste buds. Without waiting for Cici's orgasm to dissipate, he grabbed her hips and yanked her to the edge of the couch. He groaned her name as he sank into her heated depths. Once sheathed inside her, he paused, regaining the control he needed to make it last.

Movement from the doorway caught his eye. A fluttering of shadow and dark hovered at the corner of his vision and he started to turn his head.

"Fuck me," Cici demanded, wiggling her hips.

"As you wish." Davis immediately turned his attention back to the young woman impaled on his cock. He pulled out and then snapped his hips forward, eliciting a squeal from his girlfriend. He thrust hard and fast, making Cici's full breasts jiggle with every movement. When he flicked his finger over her clit, she screamed and came for the second time. Davis moved faster, pushing himself towards his own release, all thoughts of a lengthy fucking flying away.

The lamp from the end table crashed to the floor and they both jumped, Davis instinctively hunching over Cici, his own pleasure forgotten.

"What the hell was that?" Cici stared at the remains of the shattered lamp.

Davis didn't answer at first, eyes darting everywhere, searching for something. He stood, letting his cock slide from Cici's cunt. He walked to the doorway and peered back towards the lobby. For several minutes, the only sounds were the rain against the windows and the crackling of the fire. Then Davis walked back to the sofa where Cici was now kneeling, watching him.

"That was weird, right?" Davis stood over Cici.

"A bit," Cici agreed. Then, with a wicked grin, she reached out and grabbed Davis's flagging cock. His yelp of surprise quickly turned into a moan of delight. Cici brought him back to full size with just a few expert strokes. "I think we were interrupted before you got to have any fun."

"I had some fun," Davis quipped. He wrapped his arms around Cici's waist and turned her around so that her face was away from him. "But, not quite enough."

Cici placed her hands on the back of the couch as Davis positioned himself at her still-wet pussy. He slammed himself home and she grunted with the force of his thrust. Davis scraped his teeth over her shoulder as Cici snaked one hand underneath her, frantically rubbing at her clit. Before tonight, it had been almost a week since she and Davis had had time for more than a quickie. She desperately needed to cum again, and again. She screamed as her climax washed over her, bucking back against Davis who fucked her even harder.

"What's that, three so far?" Davis's words were breathless. He always talked when he was close. Cici nodded but didn't speak. She was a screamer, but not a talker. Davis liked words, liked the way they made her ever wetter, made her cunt tighten around him, made her cum harder than she ever thought possible.

Davis grabbed her breasts, squeezing them just hard enough to send little jolts of pain and pleasure through every cell. "Does it turn you on to fuck here, to know that we're screwing somewhere that may be haunted? I think it does. I think you love the feel of my fat cock pounding into you, pushing you towards a fourth orgasm, knowing all the time that a ghost could appear out of nowhere. That's what I think." He punctuated his words with short, brutal thrusts, making Cici cry out in pleasure with each one.

"Yes!" Cici forced the word out.

Davis slammed into her harder, rocking the sofa back on its legs so that they crashed down each time he pulled back. "Now, you're going to cum when I tell you to, like a good little girl, aren't you?" She nodded, unable to do more than tighten her grip on the back of the sofa and hold on. "And when you cum, you're going to squeeze that tight little cunt around my cock until I empty myself inside you."

Cici nodded again, entire body tensing in anticipation.

Davis thrust once, twice more before burying himself to the hilt and ordering, "Cum!"

Cici keened the sound ripping from her throat as she came. Her body writhed and shook, muscles spasming with the strength of her orgasm. Davis called out her name as he came, hips involuntarily bucking, forcing him even deeper inside and wringing the last of the sound from Cici's scream. They collapsed in a heap on the couch, arms and legs entwined as they drifted off to sleep.

Neither one saw the pale white figure pass by, barely giving them a glance as it floated through the parlor wall and into the kitchen.

The storm had broken before dawn, the fire had died and their clothes were dry. Cici and Davis dressed quickly, wanting nothing more than to find a real hotel with showers and electricity, maybe one nearby so they could investigate the Lightning Post further. Their skin was coated with sweat and dust, their clothes equally as grungy. As they got into the car, they remembered the strange things they'd seen the night before and both agreed that perhaps this was a real haunting. Neither one of them looked back as they started down the winding driveway. If they had, they might have seen the pale face watching at the window. The face that slowly faded into nothing as their car disappeared from sight.

## 6 FULL MOON

They could feel its pull even as they circled the dance floor, the clear, primal call to shift and kill and eat. Like the rest of their kind, wolf and leopard alike, they knew the only way to stave off the hunger for blood was to convert it to another type of hunger. And so, each time the moon reached its fullest, the Weres would prowl the nearby cities, searching for a different kind of prey. Those who had mated would disappear into the hills and forests first, not needing to find a partner. The rest, once they had sated their lust, would join their respective packs for the change.

Nineteen year old best friends Mia Dahl and Iani Belle had claimed the Purple Turtle, a local college hangout, as their hunting grounds. As the only children of their respective Were pack leaders, they were royalty among their kind and no one begrudged the princesses their right of first choice.

Mia was the elder by a few days and usually took the lead in their hunts. She wore her walnut brown hair long and straight. Her eyes were the deep brown of the rich earth. Her average height and athletic figure did nothing to indicate the sheer strength she possessed. Even when in wolf form, she was stronger than many of the others in her pack. She was beautiful, but in a way far different from her friend.

Iani was leaner; more of the feline grace associated with her leopard self, with delicate features that were often at odds with her animal nature. She kept her copper curls short and chose to dress herself in slinky clothes, always shades that complimented her hair and grass green eyes. Mia generally rolled her eyes at her friend's attire, commenting that they didn't actually intend to be wearing clothes very long when they went hunting. Iani would then retort with some mocking comment regarding Mia's simple sundress. The banter was as familiar as the rest of the dance.

Tonight was no different. The girls' eyes scanned the crowd, senses already enhanced by the coming change. They spotted two young men at a table, beers in hand, and exchanged glances. Without having to say a word, they started towards the pair. When they were only a few feet away, the men looked up.

One was tall and lean, with dark red hair and bright green eyes. He had a rebellious set to his jaw and a glint in his eyes that said he'd be up for anything. His friend was shorter with broader shoulders and thick brown hair. His eyes were a dark bluish-gray, darker still with things that made the girls' hearts beat faster.

Mia, as always, took the initiative. She leaned down close to the red-head's ear. Iani heard the werewolf clearly, even over the pounding music. "Wanna get out of here?"

"What do you have in mind?" It was the taller man who spoke, though two sets of eyes brightened considerably.

Mia grinned and let Iani take that question.

The were leopard shifted slightly to give the men a better view of her figure. The hemline of her skin-tight dress barely covered the tops of her thighs, the plunging neckline leaving little to the imagination. Every straight man in the room had been staring from the moment the girls had walked in. Iani leaned down between the men, hands on their table.

"We were thinking sweaty, hot sex in the apartment we have just around the corner."

Iani turned and Mia followed, two sets of hips swaying, neither one bothering to look back to see if the men were following. There was no need. Both were on their feet before the women had gone more than a few steps. Once outside the club, Iani fell back a step, letting the men decide who would walk with whom. Not that it really mattered. The girls fully intended to have both of them before the night was over. Weres were born, not made, and rarely got sick, never with any sexually transmitted disease. And since pregnancy was impossible with a human, they made the perfect partners during a full moon where urgency often overcame common sense.

The redhead picked up his pace until he was matching Mia step for step. "I'm Reb James."

Mia smiled and offered her name. Again, not that it mattered. Were nobility had a few extra abilities, one of which was the ability to wipe memories. Iani and Mia were more skilled than others and were able to completely erase any memory of them from their conquests, a handy little trick since they trolled the same area month after month and didn't want to get a reputation.

"I'm Iani Belle," the were leopard offered

her name first.

"Stefan Gray," the other man answered.

He was definitely going to be the strong silent type. Well, Iani mused, he would be until she had him. She'd never yet failed to make a man scream when she put her mind to it.

Before the door closed, Iani and Mia were tearing off the men's clothes, ignoring their protests at the occasional rip. If either man found the apartment's lack of real furniture odd, neither said anything. Then again, when two attractive women were in the process of undressing you and themselves, little things like décor seemed unimportant. A giant bed, devoid of all but sheets and a few pillows, stood against one wall. A couch took up space on the opposite side. The carpet was thick and lush underfoot. The only other thing in the room was a wooden box, about a foot high. This, though its contents weren't visible, contained toys that Mia and Iani themselves had picked out. This wasn't their home, just a place to play.

"We're going to do this here?" Reb cast a glance towards the other pair.

"Is that a problem?" Mia yanked her dress over her head, revealing small breasts and narrow hips. Her skin was smooth and hairless. Oddly enough, Weres in human form actually had less body hair than regular humans, not more.

Reb shook his head, all attention now on the woman in front of him. His cock, impressive enough soft, now stood at half-mast. When Mia licked her lips, the blood surged downward, swelling him to an even greater size. As usual, Mia took her conquest to the couch, leading him with one strong hand around his wrist. She shoved him back and he sat. She dropped to her knees, nipples rubbing against Reb's legs as she bent over him. She took him in her mouth, reveling in the groans spilling from his mouth as her tongue ran over his shaft.

Iani and Stefan had fallen into bed, hands exploring each other's bare flesh. Stefan was thick and hot in her hand, thicker than Reb, though not as long. Iani pushed Stefan onto his back, spinning around with all the speed of her feline self. She put a knee on either side of Stefan's head. As she lowered her head over his swollen member, she felt his hands on her hips, moving her cunt over his eager mouth. She gave a satisfied sigh as Stefan's tongue dipped inside her pussy. When she wrapped her lips around his leaking head, Stefan's moan of pleasure vibrated through her every cell.

Back on the couch, Mia had Reb hard and ready as he slipped from her mouth. Before Reb could protest, Mia was straddling his lap, pussy hovering just over his throbbing shaft. Air hissed from between her teeth as she sank down onto him.

"Fuck, you're tight," Rob groaned, fingers clenching around Mia's waist.

Mia grinned, grinding her pelvis down against him until his crown bumped her cervix. She shivered in pleasure. Using the considerable strength in her legs, Mia began to ride him.

"Shit, Iani," Stefan growled from the bed.

Iani relaxed her throat, allowing her to take Stefan's entire dick in her mouth, the head nudging the back of her throat. She wriggled her hips, reminding Stefan that he had a job to do too. He immediately resumed his ministrations, eating her out with an intensity that soon had her cumming. Sensing the man beneath her was close, Iani reluctantly rolled off of him. She wanted him inside her the first time he came. Iani slipped two fingers into her pussy, shuddering as a mini orgasm rolled over her.

Stefan had opened his mouth to complain when Iani had released him, his cock waving in the air, almost purple with need. Instead, the words dried up in his mouth as he watched Iani take her fingers, coated in her own juices, and slide them into her ass. Her eyes locked with his as he realized what was being offered.

Sparks of gold shot through Iani's irises as she worked her fingers into her ass, stretching herself enough to take Stefan's cock with just the right amount of pain.

"You're going to scream for me," Iani's voice was rough as she pulled herself up on her knees.

Stefan stared, eyes wide, as Iani positioned herself and began slowly lowering herself, sliding his cock into her ass an inch at a time. He made a strangled noise in his throat as her muscles contracted around him and fought the urge to cum. His fingers tightened on the sheets as Iani began to squeeze his length, moving her hips in small circular motions. When she began to bounce, his hands went to her full breasts, rolling her nipples in his fingers. She arched against him, nearly purring with pleasure.

"My clit," Iani ordered as she worked him and he dropped a hand to obey. The heat in her belly spread and she knew she was close. Her nose twitched and the change in Stefan's pheromone levels told her that he was ready too. She increased her pace, forcing him deep inside at a rate that was almost painful. His fingers rubbed at her clit even faster and Iani leaned back slightly, letting one hand fall back between Stefan's legs. The moment she felt her climax start, she pushed just the tip of her finger into his ass and

Stefan's back arched as he exploded, screaming her name. Iani rode him through her own orgasm, milking the last drop of cum from his cock.

As she dropped down onto his chest, she whispered, "Told you I'd make you scream."

Mia pressed Reb's mouth against her breast as they came together, the sensation of his teeth scraping over her sensitive nipples giving her the final push she needed to climax. She rested her forehead against the back of his head while she waited for her breathing to slow. Finally, she climbed off of him and, on shaky legs, padded off towards the bathroom. Iani followed and the girls returned just minutes later, washcloths in hand. Iani went to Reb and Mia to Stefan. Without a word, the girls wiped down the half-passed out men, using the excuse to bring them back to full hardness. By the time the girls finished, the young men were staring down at them, unsure about what was going to happen next.

"We're not quite done with you," Mia smiled at Stefan. She ran her hand over his cock and he groaned. It felt good, too good, too soon, but Mia didn't give him the time to rest. After a few more strokes, she climbed onto the bed and faced away from him on all fours. She looked over her shoulder. "Come on then. Let's see if you can fuck pussy as well as you can ass."

Stefan looked over to where Iani had positioned herself on her back, one leg hooked over the back of the couch. Reb was kneeling between the young woman's legs and glanced at his friend as well. Reb raised an eyebrow in question and Stefan shrugged.

"Let's go, guys," Iani prompted. "It's not rocket science."

"Make it quick and hard," Mia instructed. "We've got somewhere to be and need to cum at least one more time."

"Where do you..." Stefan started to ask.

Reb cut him off. "Really, asshat? That's your response?"

Iani's chuckle turned into a cry of pleasure as Reb buried himself to the hilt in one thrust. He didn't waste any time, pumping his full length in and out in deep, long strokes. His mouth worked at her neck, leaving bruise-like marks on her pale flesh, and she raked at his back with her nails. Vaguely, Iani was aware of the other couple, but their presence was a phantom in the back of her mind. Stronger still was the pull of the cresting moon and she knew they didn't have long before the shift would be forced on them. She needed to cum again, and soon.

"Harder," she commanded, digging her nails in hard enough to draw blood. "Come on, fuck me harder."

Reb complied, grunting with the force he put behind each thrust. He straightened, using his hands on her hips as leverage to go deeper. Iani keened as his cock passed over her g-spot and he immediately repeated the movement. Sweat poured from his body as he fucked into Iani with bruising force. Her cunt contracted as she climaxed, but he didn't stop, letting her scream and buck against him as he shoved his cock through her convulsing walls, never letting her over stimulated body rest.

On the bed, Mia was encouraging Stefan as he thrust into her from behind, his thick cock stretching her pussy, rubbing against every inch of her insides. "That's it, right there," Mia pushed her butt back against him, forcing him deeper into her pussy. "Fuck me, Stefan. You can do it harder. Come on. I want it harder. I'm not going to break."

Stefan bent forward, reaching underneath Mia to grab her breasts. His movement shifted the angle and Mia growled, fingers digging into the bed with enough force to tear through the mattress. Not that it mattered. It wouldn't be the first time they'd need to repair the apartment after a full moon.

"Fuck me so I'll feel it," Mia's voice had gone low and she knew her eyes were flashing from her normal brown to the russet color she had in wolf form. The change was close and so was her climax.

Stefan snapped his hips forward and Mia called out his name, cumming as his cock hit just the right spot. Her arms dropped out from under her and Stefan used the opportunity to wrap his hand in her thick hair. Mia's mouth opened in a silent scream as he drove into her again and again, tugging on her hair with just the right pressure to make every cell in her body dance the line of pain and pleasure, the latter winning out as he rode her through one orgasm and into the next.

The men came within seconds of each other, emptying themselves into the women with nearly identical groans. Reb collapsed onto Iani as Stefan rolled to one side, breaths coming in deep drags. Once their heart rates had dropped back down to normal, Iani and Mia exchanged looks. They may both have still been a bit weak-kneed, but they had to go. If they stayed any longer, they risked turning and, even with their usual appetite curbed for the night, the temptation would be too great if the men were just lying there, vulnerable.

Iani ran her hand over Reb's hair, down the back of his neck and the length of his back, murmuring in his ear as she erased his memory. Mia knelt over Stefan, eyes locking with his as she ran her fingers through his hair, across his cheek and gently traced his lips with her fingertips. She didn't speak, but let her thoughts bleed into his, eliminating their faces and names from his memory. His eyes slipped closed and Mia climbed off of the bed.

"Ready?" Iani asked, reaching for her dress.

Mia nodded, sliding her dress over her head. "Pity we had to wipe them. They were fun."

"Maybe next month we can do them again," Iani shrugged. "Well, again for us. The first time for them."

With a last glance back at the sleeping men, the girls slipped from their apartment. The men would wake at sunrise, still half-dazed, with only the hazy memory of hot sex with two strangers. By the time they reached their home, they wouldn't be able to recall where they'd woken up or even where they'd met their mysterious hookup. The girls would spend the night in the forests with their packs, shifting back only as the sun rose. After a few hours of sleep, they and the rest of their kind would return to the lives they lived every other day of the month, all the while knowing the next full moon was approaching and the process would need to repeat itself.

# 7 WILD HORSES

The afternoon sunlight streamed in through the wide door at the end of the loft, casting a warm glow across the hay and the writhing figures upon it. All three were naked, bodies covered in a sheen of sweat, a crown tossed on top of the clothes piled in the corner, long forgotten. None of the trio spoke, the only noise their sounds of pleasure and the slick slide of flesh against flesh.

The woman's light blond hair had been pulled back in a braid that was now littered with pieces of hay. The man at her head had the braid wrapped around his hand as he thrust his cock into her eager mouth. His golden blond hair was plastered to his face, hazel irises barely visible around the black. Between her spread legs was a dark-haired man, face pressed up against her. When he sat up, the woman made a protesting sound around her mouthful. She immediately gave a sigh of satisfaction as the brunette slid his dick into her waiting cunt. The blond at her head ceased thrusting, instead allowing the other man's movements to push the woman's mouth further down his swollen shaft.

After a few minutes, the blond slid out of the woman's mouth with a soft pop. The brunette wrapped his arms around the woman's waist and rolled over, putting her on top. The blond grinned, sidling up behind the pair as the woman began to ride the man beneath her. The dark-haired man pulled the woman down against him, stilling the movements of their hips. The woman whimpered, squirming, against him.

The blonde knelt between the other man's legs and leaned forward. His tongue circled her hole, teasing the tip past the ring of muscle. She groaned as he pushed his tongue inside and then followed it with a finger. With the practiced ease of one accustomed to the situation, the blond positioned himself behind the woman and pressed the head of his cock against her asshole. The sound that fell from her lips as he began to inch his way inside was part pain, part pleasure. Her nails dug into the dark-haired man's arms, leaving red crescent marks on his tanned flesh. When the blonde man's balls came to rest against the woman's ass, both men held their positions, letting the woman adjust to the intrusion. Without a word, the men began to move together, their movements synchronized so that when one withdrew, the other would push forward. The woman grunted as the men's thrusts started coming faster, their rhythm faltering. The scent of sex mingled with the smell of fresh hay as the trio rocketed towards their orgasms.

The woman came first, bucking and screaming as the pleasure overwhelmed her. The men continued to pound into her even as her internal muscles spasmed around them. The brunette came next, cursing as he spilled into her, her pussy milking the last drop from his cock. The blond lasted only seconds longer before emptying himself into her ass. The trio collapsed into a heap, the woman sandwiched between the two men. Gradually, their ragged breathing slowed. Finally, the woman sighed and sat up.

"I hate to fuck and run, boys, but my father and mother have ordered me to the throne room at dusk," her pale blue eyes glowed in the fading light. "Brock, please make sure the grooms rubbed down White Dream. They forgot last time."

"Of course, Princess Valeria," the blonde smiled.

"And, Harry," Princess Valeria turned her attention to the dark-haired man. "Do not forget that my mother wants three new rose bushes in the gardens by week's end."

"Yes, Princess,"

"And now," Valeria stood. "I need to clean up. Somehow I doubt my parents would approve of me arriving smelling of hay and sex."

Nineteen year old Katherine of Shada glowered at her reflection in the mirror. The arrival of her sister's betrothed had the castle in a tizzy and now everyone expected her to dress appropriately. She didn't understand the need. After all, Prince Jashua of Kalvo wasn't coming to see her. Still, her parents had insisted on her presence and followed that up with an order to wear attire in accordance with her station, which was why she now found herself in an elegant silk dress the same dark green color as her eyes. Behind Kat, her personal maid Jia, patiently picked the last of the tangles from the princess's hair. The heavy bittersweet-colored waves required more attention than Kat cared to pay and it was only the threat of losing her favorite horse that kept her from cutting it all off.

"Almost done, Princess," Jia commented as the princess fidgeted. "I'll have it pinned up and out of your way in a moment."

Kat sighed. It wasn't Jia's fault she had to play the dutiful daughter at court rather than being out and about in the palace grounds. Her preference for rough, outdoor activities had been a constant point of contention between her parents and herself. It was only her occasional consent for things such as this that kept the arguments from getting truly out of hand.

The knock at the door came too soon and Kat grimaced. Might as well get it over with, she supposed. After all, Valeria would be the one spending time with the prince. Once the official introductions were done, Kat could return to her usual activities. Or, at least, she hoped.

When twenty-one year-old Jashua of Kalvo entered the Shada throne room, his outward appearance was everything a prince should be. His clothes were perfect, his movements graceful and strong. His face betrayed none of the turmoil raging inside him. He hadn't wanted to come to Shada, hadn't wanted to be forced into a marriage with a woman he'd never met. But Kalvo was a small kingdom and he was its only heir. An alliance with a large domain like Shada would ensure the safety of his people. And whatever feelings Jashua may have had about being married off against his will paled in comparison to what would happen to Kalvo without strong allies.

He gave his rehearsed speech with practiced ease, the flowery words of royalty flowing easily off his tongue. Then it was his turn to listen as the king and queen introduced their children.

"Prince Gendry." The crown prince was only twelve but already had the telling bearing of one being groomed for the throne.

"Prince Tomas." The youngest of the royal family fidgeted uncomfortably in his dress clothes.

"Princess Katherine." The red-haired girl looked distinctively uncomfortable.

"And, of course, your lady, Princess Valeria." The king smiled.

Jashua gave a slight bow towards the beautiful blond princess. She sent a dazzling smile his way, but he noticed that it didn't quite reach her cold blue eyes. He immediately sensed that he would have no warmth from this one and repressed a sigh. He'd truly hoped that his betrothed would at least have been willing to work out a friendship. He felt eyes on him, one gaze heavier than the others. Out of the corner of his eye, he noticed the younger princess watching him, the light in her green eyes far more intelligent than he'd first realized.

Kat studied the prince with interest. He was more handsome than she'd imagined. Not that she'd really put much effort into picturing her future brother-in-law. He was tall, a full head taller than Kat herself. He would tower over Valeria who barely came to Kat's shoulders. His hair was the blue-black of Kalvo nobility, his eyes a blue so dark it was almost black. She was so engrossed in her perusal that she almost didn't hear the king dismiss them.

She controlled her pace, keeping herself to a ladylike walk until she exited the throne room. It was only then that she broke into a run, eager to be out of the expensive gown and into one of her simple cotton garments. It was too late for a ride, but she could still visit Shadow Dancer before it grew too late.

She'd been in the stables for over an hour when she heard footsteps behind her. When she turned, her eyes widened in surprise. Prince Jashua stood two stalls down, obviously checking on his own horses. Kat watched, intrigued. Most royalty, especially a crown prince, wouldn't have made the effort, but Jashua's expression reflected his care for his animals.

"They're magnificent creatures," Kat surprised herself with her boldness, taking a few steps towards the prince.

He visibly jumped; obviously unaware that he'd had company. "Princess Katherine," he said politely, regaining his composure quickly.

"Kat, please," Kat came to stand by Jashua, her eyes fastened on the sleek black stallion in the stall.

"Very well," Jashua relaxed ever so slightly. "I was not expecting anyone else to be here, especially not..." His voice trailed off and he flushed.

"Not a princess?" Kat grinned. "It's all right. I'm not exactly a normal princess."

Jashua resumed patting the horse's neck. When he asked his question, his tone was nonchalant, but Kat could feel the tension in each word. "And your sister? What kind of princess is she?"

Kat thought before answering. She didn't want to lie, but she couldn't tell Jashua the whole truth about Valeria. She loved her sister. She just didn't really like her very much. They were only a year apart in age, but couldn't have been more different. Finally, she decided on the truth

– just not all of it. "Valeria is exactly what a princess should be. The perfect host, always in control and composed. She excels at running the household, sewing, singing... everything a good princess should do."

"You don't?" It was half a question, half a statement.

Kat shook her head. "I've got a temper. No patience with people, just animals, and I'd rather spend my time riding Shadow Dancer than planning a dinner party."

Jashua started to speak again, another question on the tip of his tongue, when a noise outside startled them both. Kat placed a finger on her lips and motioned for Jashua to follow her. Most of the grooms had gone back to their quarters for their evening meal, leaving only the head groom, a twenty-one year old named Brock, to watch over the royal stables until the night shift came on. Kat hadn't seen Brock yet, and didn't want to wait if someone or something was trying to get into the stable. The sound was coming from the back of the stable, so Kat and Jashua made their way to the partially opened door. Kat looked out first. At first, she could see little more than two shadows, but, as her eyes adjusted to the lack of light, she clamped a hand over her mouth to keep in an exclamation.

Valeria knew that another tryst with Brock was dangerous, but as she'd spent the evening with Jashua, contemplating a future with the heir of Kalvo, all she could think about was getting Brock between her legs again. Not that she'd had to convince him. Only minutes after finding him behind the stables, she was bent over a bale of hay, skirt tossed up to expose her bare ass and Brock's fingers were thrusting into her hole.

"I'm still stretched from earlier," Valeria kept her voice low. "Just fuck me already."

"Your wish is my command, Princess," Brock grinned. He mounted her, pressing the tip of his cock against the puckered rosebud and then grabbing her hips. He paused, letting the anticipation build, and then slammed himself into her ass.

Valeria made a strangled noise that may have been intended to be a scream, cut off when she shoved her knuckles into her mouth. Every thrust jarred her forward, pulling down the front of her dress until her bare breasts was being scratched by the hay. She didn't move, letting Brock pound into her until her entire body was convulsing with pleasure.

"Guess that answers one of my questions," Jashua whispered against

Kat's ear.

"All noble daughters are trained in the art of love-making," Kat found herself repeating the Shada standard. "None come to their marriage bed a virgin."

"Not that," Jashua was suddenly aware of how close he was standing to the princess. "I'd wondered if Princess Valeria already had a lover."

"I didn't know." Kat turned and caught her breath. Jashua was only inches away, close enough that she could smell soap and spices and the faint scent of horses.

"I believe you," Jashua's voice was still low as he stared down at the princess. Unlike her sister, Kat didn't smell like flowers. The younger Shada princess had an earthier scent, not bad, just something darker than Valeria. Jashua felt himself growing hard as he reached over Kat's head and gently shut the door. "What about you?"

"What about me?" Kat swallowed. At this proximity, the prince's eyes were the same shade as the night sky.

"Do you have a lover?" Jashua had a moment to wonder why he was asking Kat the question. He was betrothed to Valeria, no matter what he'd seen outside. Then Kat's lips parted, her tongue running over her full bottom lip and he bit back a groan. He didn't want the vapid, empty-headed blond princess. He wanted this one. The one with intelligence and fire in her eyes. The one who he was sure would want to help him run his kingdom rather than sit in the castle, playing at court.

Kat shook her head. She knew what she wanted was wrong. Jashua was meant for her sister, but she couldn't stop her body's reaction to his nearness. And when he bent his head to cover her mouth with his, she didn't stop him. Her hands found themselves at the base of Jashua's neck, fingers tangling themselves in his thick hair even as one of the prince's hands maneuvered its way into the front of her dress. When his fingers found her nipple, she moaned into his mouth, lips parting to give access to his questing tongue. His teeth scraped her tongue as he moved his lips from her mouth, down her jaw line to her neck. Kat's head fell back, giving the prince access to her throat. When his mouth latched onto her nipple, she gasped and arched her back, pushing her breast towards his mouth. She was only vaguely aware of his hands gathering her skirt, pushing the material upwards until her womanhood was exposed.

"I want you," Jashua breathed against her skin. "But I will stop if you ask it of me."

Kat found the question ludicrous. Of course she didn't want him to stop. Tomorrow, she might regret her decision, but now, the throbbing between her legs needed answering. "Fuck me."

Jashua nodded, using one hand to hold her skirt while the other deftly unfastened the lacings to his pants. He pushed them down just enough to free himself. His cock arched towards his belly, already swollen and leaking. He took just a moment more to run a finger through her lips. He found her wet and ready, pushing against his hand.

"Please, Jashua," Kat pleaded, hands clinging to the prince's shoulders.

Joshua needed no further encouragement and buried himself in the princess's cunt with one stroke. Kat whimpered, head falling forward so that her forehead rested on Jashua's shoulder. He was thick and heavy between her legs, his girth stretching her far more than her previous lovers. Every movement of his hips rubbed against that delicious spot inside her and she couldn't stop her body from writhing against him.

It was no gentle love-making, no tender moment. It was rough and raw and everything both of them needed. Jashua thrust up into the princess, body pressing her against the stable door until she wasn't sure which was harder, the wood or him. She nipped at his neck and he responded with bites of his own, sparks of pain punctuating each wave of pleasure as their hips rocked together. They heard Valeria cry out her pleasure on the other side of the wall and the knowledge of what they were doing crashed over them, pushing them both the final bit they needed to climax.

Jashua rested his forehead against Kat's as they came down from their high, dragging air into their burning lungs. Jashua let himself slide out from Kat's cunt and released her skirt. As he tucked himself back into his pants, Kat adjusted her top and smoothed down her hair. After a moment, she stole a glance up at the prince.

"So, what do we do now?" Kat hoped her voice sounded stronger than she felt. While there had been something primal about their fucking, she'd felt a deeper connection with the prince. More than it should have, the thought of him marrying her sister upset her.

"Now," Jashua spoke slowly, watching Kat's face to gauge her response. "I approach your father about changing my betrothal."

Kat smiled, her entire face lighting up. "Are you sure?"

Jashua nodded. He held out a hand, threading his fingers through Kat's. "Did you know," he asked as they headed back to the palace, "that Kalvo is known for its herds of wild horses?"

Kat shook her head.

"I love to ride with them." Jashua tucked a strand of Kat's hair behind her ear. "What do you think of that?"

Kat leaned her head against Jashua's shoulder. "I think it sounds perfect."

# 8 NEEDING THE HORIZON

The man's body writhed under the tall, slender female above him. He ran his hands up her sides, cupping her bare breasts and running his thumbs over her nipples, feeling them harden under his touch. Bittersweet curls gleamed as they cascaded down her back, brushing the muscular thighs flexing beneath her.

He sat up, keeping their rhythm steady, and tried to capture her mouth with his. She pushed him back down on the bed, palms flat against the muscles of his stomach. The air was heady with sex and sweat; the only sound was their harsh breathing and skin against skin. He moved his hands to grip her hips, but she maintained control, riding him towards her pleasure. She could feel it building inside her, increasing her pace, pushing herself towards climax.

Skye Adams woke with a start, breath coming in gasps, a sheen of sweat covering her bare skin. She groaned with frustration, her aquamarine eyes staring up at the ceiling of her cabin. She ached with the need to climax and slid her hand between her legs. Her fingers slipped into her core easily, her pussy soaked from the dream. It took only a few quick strokes to send her over the edge. When she came down a few minutes later, she made a decision.

"We make for port on the Red Isle," Skye announced to her crew, and they gave a cheer before hurrying to obey. The Black Waters had been out to sea for two months, and the women were getting antsy. They'd been riding the trade routes, raiding the occasional straggler and waiting for a big score. The waters had offered nothing but disappointment as rumors started to circulate that the Golden Dawn was under a new captain. Skye had a bad feeling she knew exactly who that captain was and why the takings had been slim as of late.

"How long are we going to be at Red?" Lou Jenkins was a year older than Skye and had been the captain's first mate since the redhead had taken command two years before. Lou may have only had one eye — having lost the other as a child when a squall snapped an unsecured rope at her — but she saw more than most with two.

"Long enough," Skye grinned down at her friend.

Lou returned the smile, dark eye sparkling. She'd known Skye long enough to know it wasn't land the captain was craving. There were a few women on board who would've been more than willing to help the captain out, but Skye was a lover of men only, and it had been a while since Black Waters had been near anyone of that particular persuasion.

The winds favored Black Waters, and she anchored off the coast less than twenty-four hours later. Lou assigned shore leave rotation, leaving herself and the White twins — Dale and Day — onboard for the first day while the rest flocked to the bars and brothels that lined the Red Isle shore. Only one other ship rested in the clear waters, its crew appearing to already be onshore. Once their feet hit the sand, the crew scattered, heading for their favorite stomping grounds, eager to spend their share of the gold they'd commandeered over the last two months.

Skye made her way to The Lazy Sow, a cleaner-than-usual tavern that served surprisingly good food with their better than average beer. As she drained her second glass, a figure at the back of the room caught her eye. He was tall and tanned, his thick copper hair windswept, his grayish blue eyes staring directly at her. He raised his glass, tossed back the last gulp and stood, tossing his coin on the table. He raised one eyebrow as he walked past Skye. With a grin, she did the same and followed him outside. From the dark alley next to the tavern, a hand shot out grabbed her wrist and pulled her into the shadows.

"Brady." The name was the only word Skye got out before the young man captured her mouth with his. There was no gentleness, no tenderly exchanged kisses. It was all open and wet and tongues sliding against each other, teeth scraping over lips. Skye slipped her hand between them and cupped the hardness beneath Brady's lacings, making him moan in her mouth. He reciprocated by working his hand under her jacket and squeezing a breast through her saltwater-stained shirt.

"Back to the ship." Brady tore his lips from Skye long enough to speak four words and then latched onto her throat, sucking the skin into his mouth, tongue tasting the sea and sweat and the flavor that was Skye. She responded by grinding her hips against his, teeth nipping at his earlobe. This was what she'd been wanting.

On the deck of Black Waters, the White twins, identical women with white blond hair and dark green eyes, sat with Lou on the main deck, a worn pack of playing cards between them. All three appeared to be intently involved in their game, oblivious to the sound of three pairs of boots on the rope ladder, then sneaking across the deck.

It was Dale who broke the silence, still looking at her cards. "We have three guns pointed at you and no problem using 'em."

"Then you lovely ladies will have no one to ease the ache between yer legs."

All three women dropped their weapons as they turned towards the familiar voice.

"Dirk," Day grinned at the speaker. He was tall, lean, with sandy brown hair and sparkling blue eyes that devoured the short, curvy pirate in front of him.

"Ward," Dale gave an identical smile to the dark-haired, dark-eyed man next to

Dirk.

"How've you been, Lou?" The shortest of the men addressed the first mate. His golden hair shone in the fading light and his eyes were the green of the sea.

"Good, Tyrus."

"Now that we've got all that outta the way, can we get to what we came for?" Dirk took a step towards Day. "I ain't had a woman in months and my balls are like to bust."

Day rolled her eyes. "We're on watch. Can't leave the deck."

Dirk's grin widened. "Makes no matter to me. Plenty of room and I never mind an audience."

Day squealed as Dirk swept her up in his arms and planted a scorching kiss on her waiting mouth. They made short work of their clothes, hands and lips roaming over newly bared skin as clothes fell to the deck. The other two couples followed suit.

Tyrus lifted Lou onto a barrel, his shirt protecting her bare skin from splinters. She opened her legs, using her ankles to pull him towards her. Tyrus's cock was hard and ready, the tip nudging her opening as he bent his head to suck a dark nipple into his mouth. Lou fisted Tyrus's short hair and yanked his head up. "I'm not looking for foreplay." She reached between them, taking him in her hand and stroking him once, twice. He needed no further encouragement, burying himself in her dripping cunt. Lou dug her short nails into Tyrus's muscular ass as he started fucking her.

Meanwhile, Dirk had bent Day over the table, her ample breasts pressed against the rough wood of its top, and was pounding into her, the ruthless pace forcing the air from her lungs in short bursts. Dale was on her knees in front of Ward, his thick shaft disappearing between her lips as her hand worked between her legs, readying herself.

Brady and Skye tumbled through the door to his cabin, a trail of clothes following them to the captain's bed. Skye pushed Brady backwards and climbed onto the bed, straddling his waist, his manhood lying curved and thick against a flat, muscled stomach. She rubbed her crotch against him, letting her juices cover his cock as she leaned forward and pressed her lips to his chest. He yelped as she nipped at him, hips involuntarily jerking. She chuckled and wriggled against him, this time getting a far different response. His cock swelled beneath her, the friction on her clit making her even wetter.

"How much gold do you have, Brady?" Skye murmured and the man under her stilled. "Come on, I know you were the one leading those raids. Only your Golden Dawn could beat Black Waters."

Brady grabbed Skye's wrist, eyes flashing. "Is that why you brought me here, to interrogate me about my treasure?"

Skye rubbed her pussy on his dick and watched those beautiful grayish blue eyes roll back in Brady's head. "Don't you like my torture methods?"

"Come on, Skye, you and I both know what you want." Brady's voice was strained.

Skye used her free hand to reach under her and positioned Brady at the right angle. She slid the tip of the crown inside her, letting him feel her moist heat. "What I want? Be honest, Captain. You dream about me. About my tight, hot cunt squeezing you until you're ready to explode."

Brady made a low noise in the back of his throat. When Skye dropped down an inch and then lifted herself off him again, he swore. "Fine, you're right, okay? Golden Dawn's hit every major ship. We have enough in the hull for three lifetimes. Just fuck me, please," he begged.

Skye sunk down on him with a sigh. She hadn't been sure he would cave before she did. He stretched her in all the right ways and she began to move, letting him slide part way out before dropping back down again. This was what she'd wanted, what she needed. She closed her eyes and tossed her head, letting her legs do all the work, setting a slow, steady pace. Then Brady's thumb was on her clit and she screamed as an orgasm took her by surprise. Her body shuddered, muscles convulsing around his cock.

He took advantage of Skye's momentary stillness to grab her waist and flip them over so her back was against the mattress. He took her legs, draping them over his shoulders as he drove himself deeper into her tight channel. She cried out again as the head of his cock rubbed over a sensitive spot inside her. Brady began to thrust into Skye's cunt, her breasts jiggling with each stroke. Her fingers dug into the sheets as pleasure coursed through her, wave upon wave until it was almost too much. Brady cried out as his climax erupted out of him, his cock pulsing as her final orgasm milked the last drop of cum from him. He collapsed onto her for a moment before rolling off.

They lay on their backs, sweat glistening on their sun-kissed skin, as their breathing slowed. Skye turned her head towards her lover, watching and waiting. She'd known Brady since childhood, two of the few children to ride the seas with their fathers. They'd become lovers two years ago after her father had died. They knew their crew members spent time together as well and assumed rumors about them abounded. As long as it didn't soften them in the eyes of their people, neither one minded. Skye knew Brady's body like she knew her own. And she knew how the scene always ended. His eyelids closed and, a few minutes later, his breathing grew deep and heavy.

Skye slipped from the bed and quickly dressed. She took one of Golden Dawn's boats and rowed to her ship. Once on board, she saw a familiar sight. Lou, Dale, and Day were gathering their clothes while three members of Brady's crew searched for their own. Lou saw the captain first and caught the others' attention. The White twins and first mate minutely nodded to indicate that they understood their orders and reached for their previously discarded weapons. The men never saw them coming and were dropped to the deck with three simultaneously struck blows.

"Lou, gather the crew. Dale, Day, you're going to come with me to the Golden Dawn. She took from our raiding grounds and we're going to take back some of what should've been ours." Skye grabbed one of the men by the armpits. "We'll deposit these three in their bunks while we're there."

"Brady's going to come after us for this," Lou cautioned her captain.

Skye grinned. "Oh, I don't doubt it."

Brady groaned as he stirred. His head was pounding as it only did after a good night of drinking and sex. He opened his eyes. His bed was empty, but that didn't surprise him. Ever since he and Skye had started fucking, he always woke in an empty bed. He grabbed his pants and pulled them on. As he was lacing them, a memory from the night before hit him and he ran from his cabin, not bothering with the rest of his clothes. A quick glance over the waters showed no sign of Black Waters and his stomach dropped. He dropped into the hull and let his eyes adjust to the dimness.

"Damn you, Skye," Brady swore. He supposed he should be glad that she'd left him anything, but his crew wouldn't be happy to find that half of their hard-earned gold had vanished. "This isn't over, lover. Not by far."

## 9 CHASE THIS LIGHT

Kaiya was never entirely sure whose dream they were in. The room was simple, clean, with very little in the way of furniture. Outside there were a few grassy hills, tall trees that neither one of them recognized and a small, clear pond. A circular wooden building sat next to the pond, reasonable protection against the gentle rains that sometimes surprised them.

They met only four nights ago, but felt like it had been lifetimes. Neither one offered their true name or any personal information. Instead, they spoke of the things they loved or spent hours in silence, lying in each other's arms.

Kaiya was a Balsikian beauty with long, dark blue hair and eyes the same pale gray as the morning fog. She was tall, with generous curves and a strength that had surprised many. In her dreams, she always wore a gown of simple white cotton, her hair hanging unbound past her waist. In her short life – a mere two hundred and sixty-three years – she'd never allowed a man to see her hair out of its traditional braids. He had been the first.

Kaiya knew him as Rek. He was only a half a head taller than her with broad shoulders and strong arms. His unruly hair was a dark purple, his eyes black. His features were strong, handsome, the type of face Kaiya had always dreamed of. He'd confided that he was much younger than she, just under two hundred, though that alone marked him as nobility at least. The thinner the royal blood, the shorter the lifespan. A commoner of the same age would be nearing death. Those without a drop of royal blood never reached their two hundredth year.

It had taken Kaiya two nights to finally be convinced that Rek was real and not a figment of her imagination. He'd finally confessed that he had the ability to dream walk, though it usually required a conscious effort on his part, something he denied for their encounters.

Now, as she lay in his arms, bare skin sliding against hard muscle, Kaiya wondered how she ever could've doubted Rek''s existence.

His mouth moved against hers, tongue lightly tracing her lips and the inside of her mouth. She pressed her body against him, nipples hard and hot against his muscular chest. His manhood twitched against her leg, swelling as she shifted. Their plain cotton garments had long since been discarded and they'd overcome their shyness the night before. Each knew that the other had something on their mind, something that was pushing them into each other's arms much faster than they'd normally be comfortable with.

"Iya," Rek''s voice was low, rough with desire.

He'd been so patient, so gentle, but she knew how much it pained him. She'd originally balked at the idea of making love to someone who didn't know her real name. Then, just yesterday, her father had surprised her with the news of her pending betrothal. Her stomach clenched and it had nothing to do with the pleasant feelings Rek conjured.

"Iya," Rek repeated the name she'd given him, this time running a finger down her cheekbone. "Are you sure this is what you wish?"

Kaiya nodded, banishing thoughts of the waking world. Balsikian royalty were encouraged to explore their sexuality once they came of age. As noble aging didn't slow drastically until sexual maturity, most royals spent a good three to four hundred years with little in the way of obligation. Very rarely did any marry before the age of four hundred; rarer still were those like Kaiya who married only less than a century after being considered an adult. Once married, the partners had to agree to any activities outside of the marriage bed. Most couples remained monogamous. The vow was to the death and an unapproved liaison was punishable by such a sentence. Kaiya wanted to experience as much as she could with her mysterious man before entering into the covenant with a complete stranger.

Rek ran his hand over Kaiya's shoulder and down her arm, leaving a burning wake of desire humming through every cell. When his fingers danced down to her hip, Kaiya shivered in anticipation. She rolled over on her back, giving Rek freer access to her body. He took full advantage of her movement and caressed her breasts, long fingers gentle in their exploration. Kaiya squirmed under the intensity of Rek''s dark gaze. No one looked at her like that, not even the men in her kingdom who lusted after her. Rek's eyes held passion and worship and something darker that made her mouth dry up. His face held none of the arrogance Kaiya had always found among her peers.

"You're far away." Rek cupped Kaiya's cheek, bending his face down to brush his lips across her forehead.

Kaiya shook her head, stretching her arms up around his neck. "I'm here."

Rek smiled down at Kaiya, pushing back strands of hair that had fallen across her face. Kaiya tugged him downward, silently urging him to her. He eagerly complied, slanting his mouth over hers. She opened her lips readily, drawing his questing tongue into her mouth. Rek rolled on top of her, his weight sending shocks through every place that they touched. She buried her fingers in his thick hair, reveling in its heavy texture.

Kaiya pulled her mouth away with a gasp, sucking air into her burning lungs. "Rek," she panted.

Rek nudged her with his knee and her legs parted willingly. As he settled between them, he kissed his way down her torso, tongue and teeth marking her pale skin. When he reached the juncture of her thighs, he gave her a quick glance from under thick lashes and dropped his head between her legs.

Kaiya keened, thankful for the privacy of the dream. Her hips bucked up against his mouth as his tongue delved into her depths. She felt him grin against her and he flattened a hand on her stomach. Warmth spread through her belly as Rek ran his tongue up to her nub, drawing the little bundle of nerves into his mouth. He sucked on it, applying just enough pressure to make Kaiya writhe, muscles contracting as the pressure built within her. When he slid two fingers into her sopping core, she exploded, crying out his name. Rek lapped at her juices as she came down, sending tiny aftershocks through her system.

She made a noise of protest when Rek withdrew his hand and felt him chuckle, the rumble deep in his chest. Her eyelids fluttered open just in time to see Rek lean over her, his lean, muscled arms on either side of her head. They locked eyes even as he bumped at her entrance and slipped inside.

They breathed a simultaneous breath of relief, as if some part of them had been in pain, but they hadn't known it until it was gone. Rek''s progress was slow, giving Kaiya the time to adjust to his size. He moved with the care of one accustomed to relishing every moment of build up, every second of exquisite agony. Once fully sheathed inside, Rek dropped to his elbows, closing the gap between Kaiya's skin and his own. He captured her mouth even as he started his shallow, slow thrusts, every shift of his hips rubbing the base of his cock against her clit. His tongue mimicked his movement, dancing with Kaiya's.

Kaiya ran her hands over Rek's back, marveling at the sensation of hard muscles beneath golden skin, stopping just above the swell of his buttocks. She could feel each flex that created the delicious friction pushing her towards the edge yet again. She applied more pressure with her nails, feeling the muscles under her hands jump. Rek made a surprised sound in her mouth and increased his pace ever so slightly.

Rek pushed himself up on his hands, reluctantly breaking the kiss. He needed the leverage. Little by little, he pulled out further on each stroke before pushing back inside. The head of his cock rubbed against a spot inside Kaiya, triggering her second climax. She let out a scream of surprise as the rush of pleasure caught her off guard. Rek concentrated on the pinpricks of pain her nails were causing rather than the amazing sensation of her inner walls convulsing around him. Only through sheer willpower was he able to maintain his rhythm until Kaiya's body stopped spasming.

She opened her eyes, pupils blown wide with desire. "Your turn."

In a movement so swift Rek almost

didn't see it, Kaiya flipped them. Her hands pressed his shoulders to the ground, her hair falling around her like a dark waterfall. Using her knees as leverage, Kaiya began to raise and lower herself on Rek's cock. He stared up at her for almost a full minute, myriad emotions playing across his face. Then Kaiya used her internal muscles to squeeze him as she rode and his eyes rolled into the back of his head. A litany of curses fell from his lips and his hands flexed convulsively.

"Look at me," Kaiya commanded.

For a moment, Rek didn't think he'd be able to obey her, and then he forced his eyes open. The sight of her riding him almost made him cum right then. Her pale skin was flushed, with darker spots across her flesh from his mouth. Her full breasts bounced with every thrust, her nipples dark pebbles. Her hair half-concealed parts of her only to be flung out of the way with the next movement. He reached for her breasts, fingers rolling and teasing her sensitive nipples.

His touch sent a bolt straight to her throbbing pussy and Kaiya swore. She was so close and, more than anything, she wanted them to cum together. She rotated her hips, drawing a growl from Rek. "Together," she panted, lifting herself until he was almost completely out of her. Rek barely nodded before she dropped herself down, his length hitting deep within her.

They cried out each others' names as they came. Rek wrapped his arms around Kaiya as his seed emptied into her and he could feel her entire body twitching with the strength of her orgasm.

Kaiya bolted upright, the aftermath of climax still tingling through her. Her heart was racing, her skin covered in a light sheen of sweat. She rested her forehead against her knees and waited for her breathing to slow. A knock at the door startled her.

"Princess."

Kaiya immediately recognized the voice of Nyx, her cousin and personal handmaiden. The Balsikian had enough royal blood to still look incredibly youthful at the age of three hundred and fifty. The door opened and the petite young woman entered. Her hair was a paler shade of blue, her eyes the green of the Balsik Sea. Many noblemen had tried to wed her, but she'd refused them all. Rumors abounded that she'd once loved a soldier who died in the war. Kaiya had never asked.

"Good morning," Kaiya was relieved to hear her voice sounded normal.

"Your father has requested your

presence," Nyx threw open the curtains, letting in a stream of late morning light.

With a shock, Kaiya realized how late she'd slept. She tossed back her covers and climbed out of bed.

"The Farsot prince will be arriving shortly." Nyx didn't have to see her princess's face to know what the young woman was thinking. The marriage would bring peace to two nations, but Nyx feared what it would do to her precious cousin. Kaiya had always been headstrong and none in Balsik had ever doubted the princess's ability to lead once the king passed. Now, with a husband who was already king of his own domain, many wondered who would truly be ruling Balsik in the future.

Kaiya sighed, the pleasant glow of her dream fading as reality set in. She reached for the gown her father had made for today. If not for the circumstances, she might have loved it. The dark blue silk was the same shade as her hair, the insets of pale gray lace identical to her eyes. It showed enough skin to be fashionable and enticing but not so much that she would lose the respect of others. It fit perfectly; hugging her curves and emphasizing her height in a way that, for once, didn't make her feel uncomfortable.

Nyx brushed the princess's hair in silence, quickly weaving it into the intricate braid-work as befitted a Balsikian royal. By the time she finished, the sun had reached its zenith and Kaiya could hear the crowds gathering outside, eager for a glimpse of the Farsot prince.

"We must go." Nyx''s voice was soft.

Kaiya nodded and stood, giving herself a final, critical look in her floor-length mirror. A horn sounded from the castle gates. It was time.

Prince Marek had been in a daze since waking. If his squire, Petyr, hadn't been paying attention, he might've forgotten some important article of clothing. As it was, he barely realized what he was wearing as he followed his guards from the ship. His father had announced the betrothal just hours before he'd set sail. The journey had taken four days which wasn't enough time to adjust to the fact that he was being married off to secure peace between Farsot and Balsik. While he wanted the war to cease – he himself had lost several friends – he wasn't sure that an arranged marriage was the best way to accomplish it.

"Crown Prince Marek of Farsot, heir to the throne of the west," his herald announced him as the group passed through the castle gates. His people parted to either side, leaving him a clear path to the king.

Marek intended to keep his eyes firmly on the monarch as he approached, but a startled gasp from the king's right drew his attention. All of the grooming and preparation in the world couldn't have stopped his reaction. Jaw dropped, eyes widened and he stumbled. He managed to catch himself, but wasn't really even aware of his actions. All he saw, all he could think about, was the woman standing at the king's side.

"Rek?" The princess's voice was little more than a whisper, but he would have known it anywhere.

"Iya?"

The king looked from his daughter to the prince and back again. Confusion ran across his features. "Kaiya, do you know this man?"

The king's voice cut through Marek's stupor enough to bring the prince back to the importance of the moment. Gathering his composure, he answered. "Good King Chal of Balsik, I apologize for my behavior. I must confess, I have never beheld a beauty such as your daughter."

King Chal turned his attention back to the prince, holding out a hand. Marek took it and bowed, unable to stop himself from stealing another glance at Iya – or

Kaiya, as he supposed he ought to call her now.

"Daughter," King Chal addressed the princess. "What say you of this match now?"

Marek could hear the slight tremble in the princess's voice. "I say it pleases me much, my father."

The king smiled and motioned for Marek to follow him. "We have much to discuss, Prince Marek."

Kaiya interrupted. "Should the prince and I not spend time together as we are to be wed?"

King Chal chuckled. "I shall not keep him long, daughter. Once we have signed the treaties, the marriage will be as binding as it can be. The ceremony is a formality and for the enjoyment of the public. Your husband shall join you before nightfall."

"Until then." Marek couldn't meet Kaiya's eyes, afraid he would forget all that he had come to do.

"I will be waiting," Kaiya murmured in response.

The day passed too slowly for the prince and princess. When at last, Marek was released to be with his new bride, he fairly flew up the stairs to the princess's bedroom. But, after he'd knocked, he was struck with a moment of panic. What if she'd thought of him as a dream, nothing more? What if she didn't feel about him the way he did about her? Then the door opened and Kaiya stood before him and the love blazing in her eyes drove away any doubts he may have had.

Kaiya asked the question first. "Did you know?"

Marek shook his head. "Did you?"

Kaiya answered the same. Her second question almost caught in her throat. "Do you still want me?"

Marek reached for her, pulling him flush against her. His lips slid against hers and both felt the same relief they'd felt in their dream. He cupped the back of her head, fingers twining in her recently unbound hair, and tilted his head, deepening the kiss. When they finally broke apart, he asked, "I wanted you before I knew you and I will want you every day and night until we are no more. And even then, in the life that follows, I will want you."

Kaiya's face flushed with pleasure. "And I you, Rek... ... I mean, Marek."

"To you, my Iya," he traced an eyebrow. "I am Rek."

Kaiya smiled and tugged his head down for another kiss. They quickly divested each other of their clothes, as careless with the finery as they had been with their dream cotton. They cared nothing for the silk of cloth when they could run their hands over silken skin. The most beautiful garments in the world held none of the beauty of their beloved's body.

They tumbled to the bed together, a tangle of limbs and laughter, mouths tasting skin, fingers exploring in reality what had only previously been touched in dream. Every so often, one would exclaim at how their dream, while so vivid and perfect, had no comparison with their new reality. When Marek entered Kaiya this time, she arched up against him, sounds of pure joy bubbling from her lips. Marek held her waist as he knelt, using his arms to lift her against him even as his hips thrust into her. Every stroke made their bodies sing, their skin hum.

Kaiya had thought their love making in their dream would never have an earthly equal. Now, as wave after wave of pleasure washed over her, she knew that dream world had been just a shadow of what the waking world now had to offer her. The realization that she would have this man forever, that she would not lose him to someone unknown, brought her to climax, screaming. And Marek's mouth was there, swallowing her screams even as he spilled into her.

They fell to the bed together, bodies still entwined. Marek tugged a blanket over them. "I'll be in your dreams, Iya," he whispered, pressing his lips against her forehead.

"I'll be waiting, Rek," Kaiya managed a soft response as her eyes closed.

In minutes, husband and wife were fast asleep in each other's arms. In their dreams, they picked up where they'd left off in the waking world.

# 10 PARAMORE

Twenty-one-year old Paramore Weldon was cursed. We're not talking about a string of bad luck. She was completely and utterly cursed. It wasn't her fault really. It was her witch of a sister — and she meant that literally, not "as in rhymes with." Paramore was only a few months older than Olivia and had been twelve when Paramore's mother died, sending the half orphan to live with her father, stepmother and jealous half-sister. Things might've been okay if Olivia hadn't brought her boyfriend home days before she turned eighteen. He'd fallen and fallen hard. Unfortunately, the object of his affections hadn't been Olivia, but the quiet, reserved Paramore.

Since everyone knew that revenge was a

dish best served cold, Olivia bided her time, searching for the perfect retaliation. Just after Paramore's nineteenth birthday, Olivia cornered her half-sister and announced the details of the hex she had placed on Paramore.

"You'd better get used to being called a slut," she'd proclaimed, her tone and cadence far different than her normal way of speaking. "For if you pass four and twenty hours without sex, you will die. And once a man has had you in his bed, he will never want you again. Only true love will break this curse, but if you sleep with your true love before he confesses his love, he will hate you for all time."

Paramore had just stared, pale blue eyes wide and unbelieving. But, later that night, when she succumbed to her desire for Hiram Matthews, a college sophomore she'd been casually dating, the next morning's response had given proof of Olivia's power.

Two years later, Paramore sat on the edge of a couch during a raging frat party, cooling surveying for her nightly conquest. Her long dark hair cascaded over her bare shoulders, her exposed skin creamy and smooth. Her leather skirt was barely long enough to be called such and her white halter-top flowed in the black light. She ignored the men whose gazes seemed to slide past her. She'd already had them. Her eyes locked onto the next likely candidate. Medium height, nice ass and blond hair. Paramore sighed. She really wasn't that fond of frat boys, but they were easy. She uncrossed her long legs, stood and crossed the room. The young man's buddies saw her coming and began cat calling. She ignored them. If she were desperate tomorrow, she might need them.

She leaned over her target's shoulder, blood-red lips against his ear. "I'm horny as hell. Let's fuck."

Bluntness had its perks, as did frat boys who'd just had enough beer to be fun but not enough to be problematic.

Adler took Paramore's proffered hand, reaching across to grope her ass with the other. More cat calls. Paramore rolled her eyes and pulled Adler towards the stairs. She was vaguely aware of Adler talking, some babble about how pretty she was, as if he needed to seduce her, as if she wasn't a sure thing. She glanced at her watch. She was cutting it close tonight. The first door she opened led to an already-occupied bedroom, as did the second. She could feel the time slipping away and shoved Adler through the third door, ignoring the protests of the couple in the bed.

"I think there's already..." Adler's sentence trailed off when Paramore gave his crotch a gentle squeeze.

"I don't care." She dropped to her knees. "They can watch or get out, I don't care." A part of her remembered that there had been a time when she would've cared, but it had long since disappeared. She dragged her thoughts back to the present and pulled Adler's half-hard dick from his boxers. She felt his hand on her head as she took him in her mouth.

"Shit, she wasn't playing," another voice said. The man on the bed had apparently decided to stay.

Paramore ignored him as she worked on Adler's swelling cock. She ran her tongue up the underside as her hand gripped his base. Adler swore as Paramore let him fall out of her mouth after only a minute. She tugged his pants down a little further, taking his boxers with them.

"Floor," she ordered.

As Adler scrambled to obey, Paramore hiked up her skirt, exposing thigh-high stockings. She extracted a condom from the top of one stocking and tore the package open with her teeth. Adler was already on his back, his stiff shaft waving in the air. Paramore moved over Adler, straddling his hips.

"Can I see your tits?" Adler gasped out

as Paramore rolled the condom over his dick.

Paramore rolled her eyes. College guys were all the same. She reached behind her neck and tugged at the tie for her top. Noise to her right indicated that the couple in the bed had resumed their activity, though she could feel their eyes on her as her breasts fell free of their confines. She lifted herself so that she was directly above Adler's waiting cock. His hands grabbed at her tits, squeezing them a little harder than she normally liked, but she couldn't afford to be picky. Her nipples hardened under his fingers, and she knew she was wet, less from the attentions of the boy beneath her than from the curse. She reached under her skirt and pulled aside her panties. There was no time for preliminaries, so she lowered herself onto him, hands pressed against his still-clothed chest for balance.

"Fuck," Adler groaned as Paramore sank down, taking his entire length in one go. He was only average-sized, but there had been no prep work and Paramore was tight.

Paramore shut her eyes, feeling the stretch of initial penetration. Olivia's hex had some interesting side effects. On the plus side, Paramore was still as tight as she'd been when she was a virgin. On the down side, it meant she was still as tight as she'd been as a virgin. Big guys required foreplay, and some of what she'd had to do over the past two years had left her more than a little sore with no recovery time. Paramore waited a moment, letting Adler fondle her breasts as she adjusted to him inside her. Then she began to move. They both had to finish soon, or she'd be a dead woman. She lifted herself off him, leaving only just the tip inside and then dropped back down. Adler made a strangled noise, his hands moving from her breasts to her hips. Paramore slapped his hands away, grabbing his wrists and pressing his hands against his chest as she began to ride him. Her full breasts shook with each movement and she could hear the pair on the bed commenting.

"Look at her fucking the shit out of him." The woman's voice was low, hushed.

"I'd love to see you sucking those tits," the man commented. His partner must've liked what he said because he groaned and the bed began squeaking in earnest.

"I'm not going to last if you keep this up." Adler's voice was breathless.

Paramore just smiled down at him and increased her pace. His eyes rolled up in the back of his head as he began to raise his hips to meet her downward movement. She could feel her orgasm building and released Adler's wrists, reaching under her skirt to rub her clit. As her climax washed over her, so did a feeling of relief. She'd made it again. Her cunt contracted around Adler's cock, pushing it that last little bit it needed for him to cum. He cried out, hips jerking as he emptied himself into the condom. Paramore felt him shrinking inside her and rolled off, taking a moment to sit on the carpet and catch her breath before retying her top and getting to her feet. She straightened her underwear and smoothed down her skirt. She didn't look at either Adler or the couple on the bed as she exited the room, leaving Adler lying on the floor, eyes closed, chest heaving, and completely unaware that his partner had gone.

As she left the frat house, Paramore looked down at her watch. Fifteen minutes before midnight. She needed to go home, shower, and get some sleep before work tomorrow. She could wait until dinner to figure out who she was going to do next.

"Were you out again last night?" Paramore's roommate was already showered and eating a bowl of cereal by the time she emerged from her bedroom. His brown hair was perfectly coifed, his clothes spotless and fashionable.

"Shut up," she grumbled, tugging on the sleeve of her ratty robe.

Twenty-two year old Zayne Star rolled his green eyes. "Honey, if you don't stop these late nights, you're going to be out of a job faster than..."

"Faster than a cute guy can get you out of your clothes?" Paramore retorted as she poured herself a glass of orange juice. "That is fast."

"Bitch." Zayne stuck out his tongue.

"Takes one to know one." Paramore settled in the chair next to Zayne.

"Seriously, Paramore, I know you hate parties, so why do you always go?" Zayne put down his cup of herbal tea.

Paramore shrugged. She'd known Zayne since high school. They'd become best friends when she rescued him from a gay-basher who'd cornered him in the art room after school. Zayne had been a transfer as a senior and made no qualms about his sexuality; hence, the severely offended lacrosse player deciding to use him as a punching bag. Ironically, Zayne had run into the jock again two years later when the said jock was on the giving end of a blow job in the bathroom of a fairly sleazy gay bar. As much as she trusted Zayne, however, she hadn't told him about Olivia's curse or the resulting consequences.

"One of these days, I'm going to get you

to tell me whatever it is you think I shouldn't know." Zayne stood. "But, for right now, I need to run. I'll see you later." He kissed the top of Paramore's head, grabbed his keys and left.

Paramore finished her orange juice in silence before heading to the shower. When she checked her outfit in the mirror less than twenty minutes later, she couldn't have looked more different than she had the night before. Long dark hair was twisted up and behind her head, a few stray wisps framing her heart-shaped face. Her skirt and matching suit jacket were dark gray, and her blouse white. She still wore thigh-highs rather than hose, but since her skirt was a respectable length, the effect wasn't the same. This was the Paramore Weldon that she'd wanted to be.

She arrived at the law offices of Portman, Stiles, and Appleby with ten minutes to spare and greeted her fellow paralegals by name. She'd only been at this job for a few months but was already known as a hard worker and well-liked by many. It was the one place she'd declared off limits to herself. If she wanted to have any semblance of a normal life, she had to have a place where she'd slept with none of the men.

As she went through the day's routine, Paramore could almost pretend that she was normal, that she was like the rest of the young women researching, filing, and doing other mindless work for the higher ups. When it came time to leave, however, and the other paralegals were discussing going out for drinks to celebrate the weekend, she knew it was time to start thinking about where she was going to meet her nightly conquest.

"Paramore." One of the new paralegals, a dark-haired young man with smoky gray eyes leaned against the edge of her desk.

"Hi, Ian," Paramore said and turned slightly so she could look up at her co-worker.

"A bunch of us are going out to the Rain Tree when we get off, want to come?"

"I can't." Paramore had a sudden, terrifying vision of grabbing one of her co-workers for a quickie in the bathroom. She blurted out the first thing that came to her mind. "If I don't get the laundry done tonight, I'm going to spend the whole weekend naked." The corner of Ian's lips twitched as Paramore clapped a hand over her mouth, cheeks flaming red. "That's not what I meant!"

"It's okay," Ian assured her. "I understand." Silence fell for a moment before Ian excused himself and went back to his desk.

Paramore watched him go, thinking, not for the first time, that if Ian was gay, she'd have to introduce him to Zayne. They'd make a cute couple. When the group left several minutes later, Paramore took her time closing down her computer and gathering her things, not wanting to risk having to decline another invitation.

The apartment was empty when she got there, and a note from Zayne stated he'd gone to visit his Aunt Mellie. With a sigh, Paramore gathered her dirty clothes and headed to the Laundromat down the street. It was surprisingly empty, so she took over two machines and loaded them as she hummed along to the canned music playing over the speakers. She settled into one of the seats and waited for the wash cycle to finish. When the door opened almost an hour later, she glanced over and then did a double-take. An absolutely gorgeous man entered, a duffel bag slung over one muscular shoulder. He had thick brown hair and surprisingly bright green eyes. A tight gray T-shirt showed off a torso that had obviously required some work and a pair of almost as tight jeans showed off an impressive bulge. The cowboy boots and hat were just the icing on a very delicious cake.

"Howdy there, ma'am," the man drawled. He tipped his hat and Paramore almost giggled. "Looks like we got the place to ourselves."

Paramore glanced at her watch. She was still good for another five hours, but if she fucked this guy, she'd be able to get a good night's sleep. She smiled. "I'm Paramore."

"Sterling," he replied. He crossed to the machine next to hers, dropped his bag and held out his hand.

Instead of shaking his hand, Paramore flicked open the top couple buttons on her blouse. "I love your accent."

"Texas, darlin'." Sterling grinned, teeth flashing white against tanned skin.

Paramore reached out and ran her hand over the tight denim, feeling his dick twitch. "Why don't you go switch that sign to closed, and I'll give you a proper welcome to the city."

By the time Sterling got back, Paramore had managed to switch her clothes to the dryer and dump Sterling's duffel into a washer.

"I don't have anything," Sterling admitted sheepishly.

"I do." Paramore pulled a condom from her jacket pocket. She always kept some on her and purchased them in bulk. She'd almost gotten herself in trouble a few times when the curse first started.

"You New York women are really something," Sterling's drawl thickened.

"You have no idea." Paramore finished unbuttoning her shirt, exposing the plain white bra she'd donned that morning. She started to drop to her knees, reaching for Sterling's jeans, and stopped, puzzled when he grabbed her wrists.

"In Texas, we take care of our women," Sterling lifted Paramore and set her on the dryer. He leaned in for a kiss, catching her cheek when she turned her head. "All right, fair 'nough." He lowered his lips to her neck, making his way down to the creamy tops of her breasts.

Paramore moaned as Sterling pulled down her bra and took a nipple into his mouth. As his tongue swirled around the hardening bud, Paramore had a moment to silently agree that Texans really did treat their women well, and then Sterling's hand slid under her skirt. His fingers crept up her thigh until they reached the juncture between her legs, brushing at the crotch of her panties.

"Damn, already wet," Sterling breathed against Paramore's skin as he raised his head.

Paramore started to protest, but the words caught in her throat as Sterling dropped to his knees. He pushed her knees further apart, hiking her skirt up almost to her waist as he pulled her to the edge of the dryer. He was tall enough to be at just the right height and buried his head between her legs. He used one hand to pull aside her underwear and thrust his tongue into her wet cunt.

"Shit," Paramore grabbed onto the edge of the dryer as Sterling began to lick her. He ran his tongue from her hole up to her clit, circling it with the tip before sucking it into his mouth. One hand joined his mouth and a finger slipped inside her pussy. Paramore's knuckles whitened as she came.

Sterling pushed her orgasm further, lapping up her juices as she climaxed. As her body stopped shaking, he stood, one hand still between Paramore's legs. With his free hand, he unbuttoned and unzipped his jeans. He had to use both hands to push down his jeans and Paramore made an inarticulate noise as he removed his finger. He retrieved the condom packet from where she'd dropped it and tore it open.

Paramore forced her eyes open and found herself watching as Sterling rolled the latex over a large, curved cock, easily nine inches long and too thick for her to wrap one hand around. Sterling felt her eyes on him and paused. "Are you sure about this?"

Paramore reached down and grabbed his dick, stroking it once, twice. "Shut up and fuck me already."

Sterling grinned again, a dimple

showing in his left cheek. "Sure thing, darlin'."

He pushed the head inside and Paramore moaned. Inch by agonizing inch, he forced his way inside, Paramore's inner muscles contracting around him with each movement. By the time he was fully sheathed inside her, both were panting with the effort. He took a moment to let Paramore adjust to his size before beginning with shallow thrusts, the tip of his cock rubbing over her g-spot with each stroke. Paramore moved her hands from the dryer to his muscular arms, nails digging into his skin. The vibration of the dryer worked its way through the two joined bodies, sending electricity humming through their cells as they fucked. Sterling's strokes grew longer, deeper, and Paramore hooked her ankles at the small of his back, using her legs to increase his pace.

"I'm gonna make you cum one more time before I do." Sterling spoke through gritted teeth as he fought his body's natural urge to start pounding into the woman in front of him. He rolled Paramore's right nipple between his fingers, lightly tweaking it as he scraped his teeth over the sensitive skin of her throat.

Paramore cried out, back arching as a second climax washed over her. Her cunt tightened around Sterling, and he thrust twice more before exploding, his knees almost buckling from the force of his orgasm. He braced himself against the dryer, forehead resting on Paramore's shoulder as their breathing calmed. He pulled out, yanking his pants up enough so he could sit in one of the plastic chairs.

"Now that's what I call a warm welcome," Sterling chuckled breathlessly. He smiled at Paramore, still close enough to sex to prevent the curse's after-effects from taking hold. His disinterest wouldn't start for another ten minutes or so.

As soon as Paramore was sure that her legs would work, she climbed off of the dryer and straightened her clothes. The machine buzzed, and she busied herself with emptying her things into her baskets. By the time she was ready to go, Sterling's eyes were starting to get the glazed look that she'd come to recognize.

She'd bought herself another twenty-four hours.

Zayne kept to the shadows, knowing his roommate would be furious if she knew he was following her. He'd known something was up for a while, but he'd thought it was just a college phase. Then, she started at her new job, the one she'd always wanted, and her behavior stayed just as odd. When she'd come back from the Laundromat smelling like sex and some spicy cologne, he knew he had to find out what she was hiding. The next night, when she'd told him she was going out for a while, he'd waved good-bye and then snuck out after her. She was far enough ahead of him that he almost didn't see her slip into a tiny coffeehouse.

It took his eyes a moment to adjust. The patrons were all college students, probably art and journalism majors. Judging by the set-up, he'd stumbled into some kind of poetry reading or something. He scanned the room for Paramore and almost missed her. If he hadn't known she was wearing a dark red peasant top, he wouldn't have known it was her. She was heading for the bathrooms, dragging some dark-haired man behind her.

By the time Zayne made his way through the crowd, the pair had disappeared into the restrooms. He opened the women's restroom door first; just enough to know that it was empty. When he did the same to the men's, he heard them before he saw anything. Then his eyes widened as he took in the scene before him.

Paramore had her forearms resting on the sink, shirt and bra pushed up so that her breasts swung free. Her skirt was around her waist and the young man behind was pumping into her at what could only be described as a frantic pace. He grabbed her breasts, squeezing them as his dick slid in and out of her cunt, his balls slapping against her ass.

"Come on, Emerson, fuck me," Paramore begged. "Harder, please, I need to cum."

The encouragement seemed to spur the young man on and he wrapped one hand in Paramore's long hair, pulling her neck back at an awkward angle. She dropped one hand underneath her, rubbing at her clit as Emerson pounded into her.

Zayne could tell when she'd climaxed. Her entire body tensed, shook, and Emerson swore as her pussy spasmed around his dick. He shuddered, face contorting as he came. Zayne let the door shut and took a few steps down the hallway. A minute or so later, Emerson emerged, face red and clothes mussed. He was younger than Zayne had originally thought, probably only nineteen or so, and wearing clothes more expensive than anything in either Zayne's or Paramore's closets. When Paramore came out shortly after, Zayne took two steps and grabbed her arm.

All color drained from her face as she realized what had happened. Tears filled her eyes. "Zayne."

"We need to talk, Paramore," Zayne kept his voice firm, but gentle. "You need to tell me what's going on."

Paramore nodded, wiping her cheeks as tears spilled over. "Let's go home. I'll tell you everything. I promise."

Dawn was just breaking by the time Paramore fell silent. She wrapped her hands around her mug even though the tea had gone cold hours ago. She stared at the brown liquid, unable to meet her friend's eyes. She couldn't bear to see the disgust in his eyes at what she'd been doing.

"That bitch." Zayne set down his own mug. "I never did like her."

Paramore looked up, heart lifting at Zayne's response.

"Have you found him yet?" At Paramore's puzzled expression, Zayne clarified. "Your true love?"

Paramore shook her head. "I don't think so."

"Well, then," Zayne smiled. "I guess we just keep finding men for you until the right one comes along." He put a hand on her knee. "But, honey, at least now, you're not alone."

Paramore threw her arms around Zayne, feeling a weight she hadn't known she was carrying fall away. After two years of suffering in silence, of feeling isolated and alone, she finally had someone who knew everything about her and accepted her, loved her. It gave her hope, something she hadn't thought she'd ever have again. She could do this. With Zayne's help, she could get through this.

# AUTHOR'S NOTE

Readers: I want to expand a few of the stories to see where the characters can be explored further. If there are any of the stories that you would like to read more about again, I'd love to hear from you!

Visit my blog at www.candraaubrey.com

Join my newsletter for free exclusive previews
www.candraaubrey.com/in

Follow me on Twitter at
www.twitter.com/candraaubrey

Like my page on Facebook at
www.facebook.com/candraaubrey

Discover my books at major ebook retailers everywhere.